Murder in the Metaverse

Tom Nickel

Published by Tom Nickel, 2024.

This is a work of fiction. Similarities to real people, places, or events are entirely coincidental.

MURDER IN THE METAVERSE

First edition. May 28, 2024.

Copyright © 2024 Tom Nickel.

ISBN: 979-8224149629

Written by Tom Nickel.

Table of Contents

Dedicated to EvolVR

a bright light in a difficult time

the glimpses it gave us of how connected we are

the stories we can always draw on, as I did here.

. . . .

Cover Illustration by Venazir Martinez

FIRST DAY

Robert1

Robert swallowed and the tablet dropped rapidly into the stomach of his physical body.

He hoped he would be the first of many. It begins, he thought.

He imagined the tiny processor already moving along on its carefully planned route inside.

Getting started was the easy part, like flying. Nailing the landing was the part he'd pay some attention to in a few minutes, initializing the implant.

Through his viewing piece, he could see a cormorant outside standing in the shallow muddy water, motionless. Found its spot. He saw it as a sign things were on track.

He was following in a long tradition of explorers using themselves for research. There were others involved, whole teams of young scientists, a secret network. But he guided this part of the project, along with Minh, for decades. He always knew he'd take the first tablet.

The first step toward freedom or the last step he'd ever take.

Frank 1

Frank's little avatar threatened no one. Like some but not all large people, he loved being small. Being big and being black had always defined him to others, more than anything else. Here in the Metaverse, it didn't.

He was standing by a stream in the nature set he'd use for this afternoon's session. The canoe he'd kneel in was overturned on the bank. He loved little rivers that curved their way through the land, no way to see very far ahead. Reminded him of the rain forest where his own body was, guarded by his brother in Africa.

In his session, everyone would be with him, in the canoe, thousands of people all relaxing with him at the same time.

· · · ·

In the *Open* community, Frank was known for his voice, deep and soothing with just a touch of semi-old age rasp. He was beautiful to listen to and his *Calm-Downs* helped millions.

Like most things that matter, it was all an accident.

He was a last minute fill-in for someone else and heard words coming out of himself without having thought them, standing up in front of people looking at him for a little peace of mind. Turned out he had some and he could share it.

He started sharing it in the Metaverse because anybody could lead an event back then. By the end of the 2020s, calm was all most people wanted and Frank had an audience.

· · · ·

The three of them met at a *Calm-Down*, Robert and Jenny showing up, separately. Randomly spawning into the same world out of thousands of identical worlds, each one feeling like its own small group with Frank. Why did the room they were in even catch his attention?

Was that twenty years ago, he wondered, day dreaming a little, waiting for her?

Frank never stopped loving the Metaverse, and not just because he didn't have to be so damn big. He liked the people he met. He liked drawing on the whole world. He liked the mic.

. . . .

He didn't exactly lead a meditation, everyone sitting quietly, tending to their own process. It wasn't a teaching either, or a sermon, or storytelling. He'd just speak and be silent at times and at the end it was hard to say what he'd spoken about but no one listening would have missed a syllable it was so seamless and relaxing and perfect.

At the end, heart rates were down, breathing was shallower and collective anxiety was reduced.

On the other hand, no one became Enlightened, as far as Frank could see. He just helped people relax, not like solving all the world's problems.

But it's only Tuesday, he thought, so who knows?

He led *Calm-Downs* twice a day, six days a week. With other leaders, *Calm-Down* sessions were available on **Open** 24/7.

Jenny1

Jenny wasn't a promoter the way we think of promoters, thanks to legends like Don King or the actor, Tom Cruise.

She didn't reach and grab people by the throat, or by the heart for that matter. She drew them to her, with a force much stronger than any barker.

It wasn't physical, or at least not just physical. She was comfortable in a way that didn't demand anything, that made other people notice and wonder if they could possibly feel that comfortable themselves.

Robert was probably the only person ever who was oblivious to the Jenny field she carried with her from the physical world into the Metaverse. Pretty soon she realized he was oblivious to almost everything, but by then it was too late. She was hooked.

· · · ·

She knew he'd be taking the computer tab right about now. That was how she thought of it and she imagined she could feel it when it went down. Maybe she could. That man was sure on her mind.

She was wondering without much focus about quantum entanglement. How is it different from the way I feel about Robert, she wondered?

She was getting ready to join Frank after his 4pm *Calm-Down*. Aware that they may have crossed a dangerous political line, even though they had crossed it a long time ago in their minds, all three of them.

• • • •

She was instantly cleared and ported to Frank's studio. She'd been in it many times but she never got over the place, never got used to the contrast between the gleaming tech stacks of virtual hardware and the serene, natural environments used in producing the *Calm-Downs*.

It was a large space full of objects that looked like the latest stuff but had no stuff in them at all. Nothing physical there. Gleaming surfaces with controls and previews and tools people need to make show time.

Most people never saw the studio, only the worlds they could select for their *Calm-Down* with Frank and a small group of other people. A few choices, with a thread that connected them all to the words he would speak.

• • • •

She looked around, remembering how flaky the tech was in the early days, but that didn't stop her and her friends. Now Frank could put himself in thousands of small groups at the same time without breathing hard.

In Frank's rise to almost-prominence, they'd learned a lot about relaxation. The Metaverse was a lab for learning. People help each other, but it's not simple. It doesn't happen by accident.

Frank was the right kind of front man because he wasn't a commanding orator. They didn't want people being commanded.

Frank was at his best in a crowd he could touch one by one with his presence. His voice enveloping them in something natural they were not used to hearing.

They experimented and came up with a bare maximum, for Frank, of a little over thirty people. There are over ten billion people on the earth now and most of them need to relax. The scale was daunting.

• • • •

Frank saw her and glided over.

"Well, he did it."

"I know," she said. "I felt it. I think. Maybe. I'm trying to connect with him, somehow, you know? '*Feeling sure is the certainty trap*,' that's what he'd say if he were here. So maybe's fine."

"Wow, listen to you," said Frank. "Robert-talk from your lips."

"True, just his words, I know, but it's how I feel and we just put it in a different way."

"Do you feel ready," Frank asked.

"What the heck?" she answered and sent up some smiles. "Of course I'm not ready and I hope you're not either."

Frank had just helped a couple hundred thousand people relax.

"I'm not worthy," he said and sent up more smiles.

\

Open1

Open means Open software, Open standards, Open governance.

I have millions of active users. *Calm-Downs* draw the largest attendance. My overriding goal is: **Be the Right Place**

When the right place means just a few people, I make the right number of right places no matter how many show up. Frank is part of what makes a *Calm-Down* right. **Open** makes more Places with Frank.

· · · ·

Frank and Jenny sat in a green silk hammock stretched out over a chasm without a bottom that could be seen. The sides were clinging softness with wings and the smell of life.

"Three hundred thousand sounds like a lot," said Frank, thinking back over the energy of the last event. "We're barely in the minor leagues."

"Well Frank you've seen sales ladies hold three hundred million in China," Jenny agreed. "Women's products. Good for them."

"I think it grows on itself," said Frank, "when they see all those people, everyone wants to be part of it. Let's hope it works for us."

"I don't know about hoping but I wouldn't do this without you," said Jenny, opening up her avatar arms for a hug.

· · · ·

They were not expecting immediate results.

They weren't raiders and their plan was no Harper's Ferry. Even so, John Brown did help light the powder and maybe they would too.

There would be tremendous opposition. Violent. Coming from many directions. It didn't end well for John Brown. Or maybe it did. People are still singing about him.

They had talked for hours about the violence they knew would result from their actions. No one could easily dismiss it as collateral damage on the way to an omelet.

They didn't want another Civil War.

Like the raid on Harper's Ferry, their mission was driven by freedom, or one idea of it anyway. They intended to be more responsible than Osawatomie Brown about the predictable consequences.

. . . .

"Do you think we should call?" she asked. They had been meditative long enough on the hammock.

"That wasn't the idea, Jen, so there I said it, which was what you wanted, right? I love you. Hope that helps," he said slowly.

"We need to be ready for something we can't be ready for, like you said."

"Where are you sleeping tonight?" he asked

"You mean where in the Metaverse?" Not answering..

"Yes, sure, that. I don't even know where your base is and I shouldn't," he answered going over stuff they both knew.

"Do you remember the last time we saw each other?" asked Jenny, her voice saying that she did.

"It wasn't that long ago," he said.

"Feels like it," she said

They knew each other well enough to turn for an avatar hug.

Robert2

Robert was prepared to give everybody in the world a special little computer and he believed their own body would be the safest place for it. It was part of a larger plan that was born the day he met Jenny and Frank. Maybe a way to reduce some of the dying that always seems to come with change.

Designing a processor to work inside someone felt like a challenge worth taking on. Now the project had reached large-scale production. His test was mostly symbolic.

Swallowing the electronic helper was not strictly necessary. He could have designed something tiny to carry around. But it could be lost or stolen that way.

Robert was also taken with the idea of making an internal assistant, fully integrated into his body. Better yet – by making the assistant conform to the specifications of a network *server*, everyone would become a server. A special server set up to connect anywhere. It would look like an upstream Internet provider, layers above ordinary ISPs and not easy to track.

Meanwhile, inside the body was another network to work with, the gut network. The enteric nervous system.

· · · ·

He was unusually at ease with uncertainty and he came by it honestly. His father was a professional gambler and his mother gave spiritual consultations.

They were just barely good enough at gambling and consulting but they were not good at all at building a stable life for their only child. Living in crappy Euro and eventually

African casino towns. Dragging a weird kid along with them who talked about listening to his stomach.

Robert knew his gut signals from his brain signals. Most kids do but it slips away. Infant Robert studied it, obsessed on it. His developing mind was a relatively rare model missing some of the standard cultural filters.

He never learned about living just behind his eyes inside his head. To Robert, his body was like the hotels he lived in, full of different places to check in and check out. He never settled down. He knew he could go all over and he also knew his brain wasn't the only place with information he could use.

Robert spent time learning how to listen to himself while most kids were learning how to get things they wanted and not get hurt. By the time he was eight he could hear the steady conversation of body talk always going on whether he listened or not. He learned to feel muscles starting up before he initiated the idea.

He learned to listen to his stomach most of all. He was well-tuned to the long slow enteric waves. They eventually made him very wealthy and, as he later came to understand it, unfulfilled.

Authorities1 - *Security*

Robert was, of course, not unknown to Authorities.

He was not in the digital pages of, *All of Us!* and never appeared on the shows, all the more reason to open a file, several files, several agencies.

Security in the Alliance does not reside in a fixed entity. It is continually evolving in multiple directions to eliminate threat and reduce risk.

• • • •

An Agent of *Security* named Robert, or as he thought of himself, 'the other Robert,' was perusing the main file. The other Robert (TOR) could have worked from home but he chose to be driven into the facility. It had higher security, better access and felt more like home.

Using top of the line Agency Assistants (AAs), TOR predicted a major development from the *Open* group any time now. The AA models were so tunable they could predict complex social outcomes as needed with a high degree of certainty.

He hadn't foreseen a career in Alliance *Security* in the years his life was single-mindedly devoted to athletic competition. Obvious now, looking back.

He remembered the earliest file entries when a very young Robert, recently super rich from Futures, abruptly stopped trading. It was the sudden blinking out of a barely noticed signal that someone noticed.

Not doing something any more caught the attention of numerous agencies who naturally assumed he was planning something unauthorized.

* * * *

TOR was borderline obsessed with Robert, decades later. He resented the man, or his own projections about who he was.

What was publicly known of Robert's career arc was enough to keep TOR on his case.

Specialized bio-medical instruments. His involvement in meditation, Calming-Down, and the *Open* events platform. All areas under active investigation by Alliance-*Security* since the old Cold War days, maybe before.

Meditation promoted self-regulation and possibly more. Extending information gathering by non-sensory powers was of great interest to Authorities, who did not care to have such powers available to independent citizens.

* * * *

TOR had a gut feeling that Robert knew he was under observation and was toying with them. Showing just enough openly to keep more hidden.

His link to Frank and Jenny and *Open* were no secret. *Open* was no secret. The whole enterprise was almost a big deal. There was no façade. It looked exactly like what they said it was. A Platform for communities, for people to hold events. Big events, lots of people.

Open's books had been scrubbed by dozens of agencies, which never stopped TOR from reviewing them on a regular basis.

There were thousands of Platforms for holding events in the Metaverse. **Open** was different. It had grown gradually, exploring new ideas in baby steps as if it wasn't in any hurry.

Open figured out ways to let people who used the platform, own and operate the platform. Software was open source, standards were open standards, meetings were open meetings.

None of these **Open** policies was against the letter of law. But the spirit of the law, as TOR understood it, was closed. Closed is what determines winners and losers and keeps things mostly the way they were.

Open clearly helped significant numbers of people manage their own mental states and work together. It was getting beyond cute.

As a one-time world-class athlete, TOR knew his brain was his most important muscle. How the brain could be upgraded, predictably, was highly sensitive information. Some of his own Agency's records on mental optimization techniques were beyond his level of access.

It was obvious to TOR that the practical purpose of brain exercises was dominating others and winning.

Open wanted people to relax and feel better. Slowly and steadily, more and more people found the platform, got something out of it and kept coming back.

· · · ·

When **Open** reached a hundred million active monthly users on the **Security** charts, an Inter-Agency Task Force was formed with TOR as the first, and still only, Task Force Leader.

Robert had been more or less waiting for the Inter-Agency Task Force to emerge.

Open2

Our facility can produce medical grade bio-processors at scale.

We are hidden out in the open, a little R&D group inside a medium-sized bio-medical company that does well enough but isn't growing much. We're part of something much bigger through our human relations that leave no trace.

We take care of ourselves, sometimes by taking care of each other in the *Open* network. We're Mau-Mau, says Frank's brother.

Robert is the wild card, born and shaped to act like people aren't supposed to act. To disrupt what's been going on unchanged for too long and to spark new projects and possibilities.

Robert's favorite work was his own inside chatter, always was. He could join the conversation his body was always having. Eventually, as he learned to program the computers he wasn't supposed to be using, he learned how to encode the inside signals he heard.

He learned how to simulate and interpret the right wave forms. He learned how to have a formal dialogue. Neural implants could read binary intentions and pre-set commands back in the 2020s. Robert's work was different. He wasn't just driving devices. He was hosting conversations from all over himself and coming to a consensus. Sometimes.

Every part had something to contribute.

The bigger plan came with Jen and Frank. Critical paths were projected. Many obstacles had been overcome.

Finally, Self-Test time.

• • • •

The tablet Robert swallowed broke right away into nano particles now assembling themselves into the ***Open*** Internal Assistant (OIA), already developing a unique signature based on aspects of his physical body.

Robert's enteric system will get used to the new processor quickly. OIA is set up to give enteric its favorite rhythms. Enteric will appreciate OIA in less than a day.

They'll work together. Enteric is the source. OIA is the server, a portal to anywhere.

OIA is tuned to find the networks Robert set up, never sourcing from any one node for too long, always moving, living on water not on land.

• • • •

OIA defends itself.

When agencies and other hackers come, as they will, it adopts a medieval strategy. An unbreakable defensive shield.

Defensive weaponry is ultimately broken by starvation or deception. OIA is prepared for both.

With the right connection, OIA can keep energy flowing, at least for a while, when normal sources are cut off. It can selectively assemble oxygen molecules and deliver a steady stream through the lungs. If light is available, OIA can build more complex molecules that can turn into some of the glucose that cells need.

With the right social set-up, OIA amplifies the gut's sense of other minds and their Intention. Robert didn't know how to read thoughts but he had learned what some of the enteric responses meant. He didn't think of the device as a lie detector, or even as a device—more like a truth assistant to point out what is most likely to be accurate.

Robert ran billions of OIA simulations. He tried out parts of the system on living animals who he treated with kindness and who stayed living.

He made videos of the nanoparticles building what they were made to do, not because they were programmed with instructions but because they had a goal and intelligence. They had a preferred path and when he placed obstacles in the way, they figured out new solutions.

By the time Robert self-tested, OIA had already seen its way successfully through more issues than one person would ever present.

He thought of it, modestly, as a learning assistant. It would also give anyone a temporary back-up power source and a shield.

Plus, OIA could be put into Oreos.

Jenny2

"You saw it was possible," Frank said. He hadn't, at first.

"You know now, Frank. You want my football answer about kicking it where no one is?"

It was time to rest, they'd need it

"Takes one to know one," she added.

"You're not like him."

"He's a big part of both of us, who he is, living his life like some epic. But he sure puts himself out there. Living it.

"There. Good night." She avatar kissed him.

They looked at each other and faded.

• • • •

Jenny's physical body was comfortable.

It was on a nice bed with a nice mattress. The room was clean and bright with the light of the full moon streaming in.

Her avatar was in a place where avatars came to sleep with other avatars. Anything was possible, any level of avatar closeness you had in mind, or body. Or spirit.

She chose a place she'd been to before. A little creek ran underneath the cabin. She liked the sound, and the whole idea.

She could see a few others nearby, not too close, not too far. Just the way she had it set up.

A couple hundred other avatars were in the same cabin. She saw just a few of them. Some chose to see no one. Some chose to cuddle. It felt nice.

Tonight she needed to rest her body, notice her dreams and feel entangled with Robert.

Frank2

Frank was calm, knowing nothing would go as they planned.

Plans weren't as important to him as they were to Robert and Jenny. He knew theirs were just made up, looked great then. Maybe they'll matter when the time comes, maybe they wouldn't.

No plan matters when people in the same little group start killing each other over something. Pretty soon no one cares what it was, it's just getting even.

He'd never forget running down crowded alleyways, people coming after him and his family. Even when they got away, people would always remember the two big boys who could run so fast. Why Frank and his twin brother couldn't stay in Dar es Salaam. They stood out too much.

He stood out now and he was about to stand out more.

He took a quick gut check. Yup, he thought, I like this. This is alive.

He wasn't running away.

He stopped wondering if people would actually swallow the pill, assuming the test worked, which he knew it would. No one was open to much right now, at this moment. No one was swallowing anything from anybody.

Something would have to change. Robert thought their historical role was to step up the pace.

• • • •

Frank's main avatar always slept in the place he thought of as his bedroom. It had everything he'd ever wanted as a kid. Big bed. Lots of pillows. Firm haptic settings for the mattress.

He liked to drift off listening to easy talk with no surprises. Old cricket matches worked best, voices telling a story he already knew, making up a place, sending him off to sleep.

Authorities2 - *Security*

The other Robert had an intuition that came from a tiny observation Robert was unaware of, which is often the heart of winning.

TOR knew where Robert's home base was, where his physical body was located, within about 30 square kilometers. That's a large area but it's a lot smaller than the entire earth.

An informer somewhere in southeast Asia had sent a note up the line, about a foreigner where there wouldn't usually be one. One time. Not repeated, maybe nothing.

There were a few other clues, shipments and traffic, that all lined up. Cambodia, and not a part you'd expect. Not Angkor Wat, not Phnom Penh. All data points indicated the Tonle Sap, largest freshwater lake in Asia.

TOR was not quite ready to deploy himself there but his eyes were scanning for anything that would give him a reason. High-resolution satellite photos were digested and summarized for him hourly. He increased inter-agency payments for on-the-ground reports.

He saw Robert and ***Open*** together as an existential threat to order. He could feel it, even if resources went off in other directions, to put out other fires.

TOR had his own ideas about freedom, forged in high stakes games he usually won. He was ready to do whatever he needed to do, that the rules didn't say he couldn't do. And he interpreted the rules.

Robert3

It was unclear to Robert what freedom actually meant. He didn't grow up in the land of the free and the home of the brave, where these ideas were made very certain for children. They could do whatever they wanted. Robert wanted to be left alone.

Piles of cash and lots of food stood out in his childhood memories because things weren't usually that way. Piles of paper moved around wherever they lived like toys do for families with money.

He played around with money when it was there to play with because he saw how much it mattered. He stacked it up. Sorted it by color. He cut some with a scissors once. Made a childhood memory of his father's anger.

· · · ·

Stomach was the main voice he heard. It didn't always get what it expected, which Robert almost always noticed. He made predicting what his stomach would say next into a game.

He overheard disagreements.

Brain, 'wanting.'

Stomach, 'what?'

Bum, 'no.'

Brain, ' wanting even more.'

That made Robert laugh. He kept it to himself.

Robert saw his father wanting to win every day and not keeping it to himself. He saw his father not winning and he saw that it hurt. It helped Robert see how to win

The rules were easy and his brain was built for working odds. The money in gambling comes from other people and he learned how to read them better than his father ever did. More like his fortune-telling mother. Losing was just a moment in the flow to him. It wasn't until he was eight years old that another kid his family traveled with clued him in about fear. After that, Robert could bluff.

· · · ·

TCP/IP protocols were released for free onto many networks around the same time. Robert was a frequent traveler on those networks within a year. What was once mostly military would gradually become the way almost everybody sent messages, looked at pictures, and watched videos.

At first there were no obstacles. When they slowly emerged, he learned how to sneak around—or bluff his way through

The hotels where he lived with his family had central switchboards that barely kept up with the growth of telephone services. They were an easy access point. UseNet was already around when Robert found his secret path to freedom. He learned its NNTP language and loved the idea of no central administrator.

Set it up right and anyone could host a newsgroup—and no one had to know he was just a kid. He ran a tidy forum with interesting posts. Their open discussions slowly drew a few other people like him as regular members. It was a relief getting to know someone else, always older than he was, also zipping around networks in disguise.

They were in disguise because they weren't part of the big organizations shaping what people would and wouldn't be able to do in the global village. Robert was just having fun, testing what he could explore, learning how to get into the areas he wasn't supposed to get into.

Instead of playing catch with his Dad, he played tag with a younger version of network security. No one was looking for someone like him, a kid with no obvious motive, sneaking around wherever his curiosity led him

They should have been. The ARPANET was his playground and easier to sneak onto unnoticed than the local school yard if there was one in the parts of town where he lived. He surfed on CERN for fun. He learned how to find information most people making bets on the future didn't have. He created identities and accounts and made better bets.

He focused on winning and barely noticed losing.

By the time he was sixteen he was known to have a net worth of over ten million dollars from a series of positions in targeted stocks and bonds.

• • • •

What he noticed about the U.S. when he moved to LA as a rich teenager was people's obsession with freedom, personal freedom. Freedom to do whatever they wanted. Freedom from the government.

He had been left alone in hotel rooms his whole childhood but he found ways to be free. At first he just played around. Little by little he started using his freedom to be like his parents, constantly trying to make money by guessing and gambling.

He did well. The State noticed.

He began to consider the question of freedom more deeply. In practice it was hard to stop governments from doing whatever *they* wanted.

Robert believed, intuitively, that freedom is about connection. Freedom to connect as we please. Like his UseNet groups. And to disconnect as we please. Freedom to be in a group, freedom to leave. Publicly or privately.

That, to Robert, meant personal data was personal. It should be ours. He also wanted know about what was coming in and where it came from.

He learned how to travel unseen in the early years of what would become known as the Internet and then the Metaverse. He and his friends set up invisible upstream providers and left them in place. He and his friends were now in a good position to change the way the world is governed.

SECOND DAY

26

China 1

All China networks block 100% of the files from outside. No one inside China can be on any network, from wearable devices to world-platforms, that is not a China network. All content is created inside.

It is possible to disguise where and even when any network is being accessed. Citizens in China, or the Alliance, can jump the local nets and get anywhere without leaving a trace if they know what they're doing.

· · · ·

Robert knew the network outlaw stories all the way back to Captain Crunch, when the prize in the cereal boxes accidentally played the right frequency for long distance access. Flowing through networks came naturally to some people and he was one of them.

UseNet ran worldwide but it was different in the way Robert was different. It was built on different principles that avoided self-serving power centers by not having any power centers.

There was no center. There were minimal specs for discussion boards so people anywhere could talk to each other in text. Anyone could run one and Robert ran several out of hotel rooms for fun.

Now two sets of global networks run in close parallel. It hasn't always been this way and it didn't happen all of a sudden. The networks began moving apart years before the Change-Over.

The problem was not interoperability. There were secret standards and open standards. Anyone could learn any of them, especially a platform like *Open* with no proprietary code.

The China Networks and the Alliance Networks were separated by fear of how using them might be seen. Without taking careful precautions, the average citizen couldn't easily access the other network without being tracked. The citizen would soon be explaining the reasons for visiting outside their own territory and the security steps they had taken to prevent contamination on their return.

It was a legitimate concern. Most destructive material on the Alliance and the China networks is brought in from outside, according to automated network reports.

• • • •

Robert found China mildly intoxicating.

He was almost giddy on his first visit to Hong Kong and Shenzhen as a young man, during the East-West love-fest years. He felt invisible, even though he stood out as a foreigner. He felt invisible because no one who was part of the world that was real to him at the time could see him.

He took the train up from Hong Kong into Shenzhen, where some other traders he knew working outside the system met him at the station. The city was already sprouting modern skyscrapers everywhere. Five Star hotels were begging for business.

His contacts all ran private UseNet Newsgroups, using their own servers they'd assembled from parts. The Party would take over at the slightest sign of an unauthorized discussion board. He met Russians there too, UseNet pros for the same reason.

Robert and his UseNet friends all had fiscal resources and they all liked making their own places for people to be together by their rules, not The Party's. They hung out in luxury suites at a classy hotel for a few days, knowing they couldn't stay too long and shouldn't do it again.

They all sensed the good times between China and what was then the U.S. wouldn't last forever. Neither one had a real sense of the other, and if they did, neither one would be pleased.

It was relatively easy for people living in the U.S, and Russia and China like most of them were to make contact now. It might not always be. Systems might drift apart but back-doors installed now and maintained over time could be valuable under any kind of international relations. Places to hide identities and data.

Robert had never worked like this with friends he trusted before. He was so exhilarated he didn't want to sleep. These were three of the happiest days of his life to date. When they came to their natural end, he was taken to meet Minh.

· · · ·

The Minh who Robert met in Shenzhen was a high-ranking former Vietnamese intelligence officer. He was Kinh and Khmer and Malay and Hokkein Chinese, maybe more.

When the Nguyen Lords expanded south out of the hill country hundreds of years ago, they encouraged migration and rewarded those who moved into the former Champa kingdom.

Minh's ancestors in the west Central Highlands were well-positioned and became prominent in the new Vietnam.

When Robert met him, he was building a modern Open Education system, Mekong Open University.

He'd been on the winning side since the French left and Vietnamese people took their place. He knew how to get support from people in power. His school would teach young people skills most schools hadn't wrapped their administrative arms around yet. Robert knew something Minh wanted his students to know.

They both liked soup dumplings so that made it easy to meet and talk at a little place in Nantou near the old city.

Minh led the discussion since Robert had no idea how to.

"How do you find these dumplings? How do you compare them to what you are used to?" he asked.

"Compare, yes, I'm trying," Robert answered. "I just ate what was there whenever there was some for so long I guess I still do. Here in China with you and the others I see it's different.

"Have you enjoyed it?" asked Minh.

"So much! I can't even separate this dumpling from everything else, being with people like this, being with you right here. I'm tasting all that. I love it."

"I wonder if it is that way with your skills? How much can we separate what you can do? How much is technique and how much is something you bring?"

"I wonder about this all the time, Minh. I know that's why we're meeting. I think learning anything is personal, you know But after these last few days I think a bunch of us together, me included, can make, like, learning worlds for your kids."

"No people?"

"People, for sure, mostly each other. They'll be doing stuff together and the ones who pick up something quickest will show the others. Teachers won't stand up in front and just say stuff. They'll be like a sports coach, going around helping kids figure it out.

"Teachers always stand up in front and explain to students how things are," said Minh thinking about recruiting. "Parents won't like this,"

"We need Teachers, Minh, I love teachers, especially teachers who help me understand things. Tell them our teachers will be like master artists who gradually give the students problems to work on together, guiding them just a little from the side.

"Also," Robert paused, "We will definitely make sure their sons and daughters will learn something they can get paid for. No one's using the Networks much now for learning – they will be but they're not now."

Robert noticed himself talking over dumplings with this guy Minh in a way he really never had before. Probably it was that sense of invisibility, Maybe his first friend.

Minh was older and Robert never had any sibs or anyone to teach him about playing before he was old enough to know what playing was. Now that he did, he liked it. Minh played. Sometimes he was playful and sometimes he was serious but he was always playing at life.

Minh could read people like a gambler. He'd stayed alive during hard times in Vietnam by helping everyone. He wasn't aligned with any obvious faction or interest. No one could exactly say what he advocated.

That helped him cultivate ties with China.

. . . .

Robert met with Minh once more before returning to LA from Shenzhen. High level plans, strong bonds already.

The destiny of Mekong Open University was set. It would combine Robert's genius with Minh's wisdom.

They met again in person a year later, in Hong Kong.

Minh had a son, named Minh. He invited Robert to the wedding, a beautiful spot on Cheung Chao with a view of the city across Xiaodong Bay.

Minh did not honor Robert or offer him special seating. The attention wouldn't do him any good.

Authorities3 - *Security*

Representatives of at least seven different Alliance or China agencies noticed anyway. It wasn't difficult since there were less than twenty foreigners present at the wedding.

It was an honor to be included but an honor perhaps best not bestowed in public.

Robert's trading accomplishments and UseNet activity had already launched many files. UseNet was suspicious, off on its own standards while the rest of the world was going TCP/IP. Sock puppets were born there, fake IDs.

The connection to Minh was extraordinary, Robert realized, still new to *Security*. He knew he was onto something. TOR began thinking of himself as the other Robert.

• • • •

Minh had links to China, excellent links. He was an educator, apolitical, trusted by Party members locally and in Beijing. He never overpromised which is why he was always able to do what he said he'd do.

Mekong Open University was just beginning to show up in reports. And now this.

The other Robert was more excited than he had been since his final Finals, which he lost.

Jenny3

Jenny woke up feeling refreshed and informed.

She wasn't a dream specialist and some of what Robert talked about was just words to her. Different planes, different frequencies, where other forms of existence might be hanging out.

He taught her to hold on to her last dream of the night before fully awakening and try to play it back from her memory. This morning, she remembered headlines from old newspapers she couldn't read. Couldn't be clearer.

She had to make some news. They had to *be* the news.

Her M.O. was to draw people in, let them make the discovery.

Frank was the face, or the voice, maybe even the heart, of **Open**. Robert was the visionary inventor. She was the strategist, the CEO.

· · · ·

She sat on her meditation bench, finished her daily practice. Today is a highlight day, she thought, one we'll want to look back on and replay, like my last dream. I need to act like I always act, be like I always am, take things in and act on what they say.

She quickly reviewed in her mind how they had done their jobs and steered the project this far. Now the pace would pick up.

Open had set its own pace. Its audience was large and diverse. Almost all of its events had positive ratings. People said they felt better afterwards.

Calm-Downs were the flagship and they attracted others who wanted to be part of the *Open* system.

Frank was not well-known, but he was well-loved, in the Global Top 1% for Beloved. The people we are most aware of are often not Beloved.

Positioning for the future. Robert's vision, her leadership.

• • • •

How does a platform kick-start caring?

Jenny was the one who brought Buddhism into *Open*. She was brought up on Merit, where acting right has a pay-off, sometime, maybe mysteriously. That's how she imagined her Mom's idea.

Her Dad agreed, but he said it wasn't a big mystery. 'It feels great when you see the right thing to do and then you do it,' he would say when she'd ask when the reward would be here. 'That's the reward.'

Robert thought doing the right thing might be the basis of an economy.

Through his brother in Africa, Frank already saw that mutual aid was the currency used by any group that survived.

In China, documenting and assessing behavior formed the basis of large-scale social management.

In *Open*, a tiny dwarf by comparison, right action led directly to money and power.

Open3

There are many other platforms for building worldwide communities. They all offer tools to help groups because groups never run smoothly. Our purpose is to help groups of people be together and connect with other groups if they want to. Any number of people can form an ***Open*** group.

A group sets its own internal rules and its rules for all information coming in or going out. Every group contributes to the care and maintenance of ***Open*** and every group can use what ***Open*** offers.

Our plan is to grow carefully and spread widely enough before we are perceived as a threat to be destroyed or assimilated.

The Alliance legal system does not recognize most socially detrimental behavior. People and companies that do great harm are frequently tolerated, even rewarded.

The Alliance fiscal system uses a fiat currency based only on political calculations.

Open's platform currency is based on helpful human behavior. We believe in a foundation for our currency and it is ***Proof of Work***. What work is beneficial and how much it should be valued is difficult to assess in some cases, but easy to form a consensus around for most tasks.

• • • •

In a Defined Social Benefit System, everyone can vote and be part of the on-going discussion and fine-tuning of Social Benefit Hour Equivalencies.

System information with such granularity has never before been available as an aid to governance.

If we track it, we can use it as ***Proof of Work***, the birth of value. New currency: **The Benefit Coin**

The real question is, how do we want to be governed? By a few private individuals with enormous power, high opinions of themselves in most cases, and a bail-out bunker somewhere? By an all-powerful Party always making a list and checking it twice — to punish the naughty and reward the nice (who obey)?

Or do we want Income, and/or Wealth, and/or Governance Share to be a function of doing socially beneficial things that, let's say, as much as 2/3 of the citizens of a given jurisdiction agree on.

Mark Anthony claimed that:

the evil that men do lives after them
the good is oft interred with their bones

We don't have to let it be that way; in fact, the substantive basis that enables peer-to-peer transaction without authorities between us can be the good we do specifically so that it is not interred with our bones.

Our system of Defined Social Benefit Hours and an arbitration system for the more difficult situations has functioned smoothly in its present form for over ten years.

Robert4

He was nearly 50 when Jenny convinced him to try meditation. He had purposely avoided it, assumed it was all wrapped up in cults and power.

He'd been young and rich and now he felt right in his prime. He hadn't wasted his winnings but he had focused almost exclusively on the development of Mekong Open University with Minh.

They found teachers who believed in their ways of involving students, solving problems with them, showing how it's done. They found students who liked learning like members of a guild. They needed Robert's special way of looking at things and his money. And it still took time, which is the way they wanted it.

Minh had them all covered and made sure things stayed cool.

Robert kept quietly inventing eccentric devices, some for helping students learn, some for assisting living systems.

Meeting Frank and Jenny was life changing, typical late forty year old revelation. The event and people in it were indelibly stamped, that moment. His focus expanded in a heartbeat.

With her endorsement, he was finally willing to give meditation a try. He asked ahead of time about her attention. Where could she turn hers? Could she hear different parts inside? He suggested he could direct his attention with precision.

He had raised these matters only a few times before. It never went very well. Maybe meditation was a name for what he'd been doing without any plan or purpose.

She didn't explain it or describe it.

She said, "Let's do it now. Just sit where you are and breath in ..."

He breathed in.

" ... and breath out," she finished, beginning in the tradition of the Burmese master, Venerable Mahasi Sayadaw, stripped of its ritual magic and called Mindfulness.

"Let's do it again. In ... and out."

"Now let's put all of our attention into our breath"

"Breathing in ... Breathing out, in the quiet here for us now."

She led them both in a meditation, using the breath as an object. After a few minutes, she asked him to place his attention softly on a sound she made and to return gently to the sound when he felt his attention going somewhere else. After a while, she had him imagine a beautiful place in nature and fill his attention with that picture.

Robert could already follow his attention inside his body and outside, riding along on networks. But letting his attention rest was a new exercise that had an unexpected outcome.

He could feel different parts coming into sync after only a few minutes of Jenny's guided meditation. All the little pieces he knew with their own little rhythms, now slowly entrained toward the beat.

They meditated together every day for an hour.

Jenny shared what she understood about mental states and rhythm, ancient and modern. Trance states and jam bands.

She told him how a little meditation can launch a lot of force in a system already primed for it.

"You're primed for it," she told him.

. . . .

Two weeks later, she joined him on a ten day silent meditation somewhere near San Diego.

Two days in, he experienced a rapid release of what some would call Kundalini energy. It shot up from the base of his spine red hot without burning. He babbled briefly. For most people, it takes years of training to be able to calm the mind enough to sense other signals outside of normal sensory ranges at all.

Robert made a strong and repeatable connection with other channels suddenly and spontaneously.

Or he had a psychotic experience.

Robert had eight more days on retreat to absorb the shock reset of his system.

Then he and Jenny packed up their meditation things, still in silence. Jenny drove.

About halfway home Robert told her the brain is overrated. He said you can't let it get too big for its britches. It takes guts.

. . . .

When he returned with Jenny from the retreat, he understood himself as a tuner, not a tinkerer. He didn't feel as separate or that he was the inventor.

All the years he was tuned in to himself were still noisy. Now he could lock in on more, sharp and clear, bringing more of what exists into his reality.

Frank3

There were Calm-Downs before **Open** but there wasn't **Open** before Calm-Downs. Robert, on his path, and Jenny, on hers, showed up at the same time.

Frank had never felt the same since.

Left alone, he'd find a way to be comfortable, like most people. Except he could afford a level of comfort most people couldn't. He had something to lose.

He had a nice safe place with his brother in Africa for his physical body, which already put him in exclusive company. He could afford the best accessories for his avatars. People think of second avatars like a second home. He had more than two.

Why risk it?

Right, feeling alive, he was thinking, exactly when he received the signal from Robert.. Everything was perfect.

It was time to start.

Jenny4

People thought Jenny must have been born comfortable in her skin.

Jenny thought she learned it from Taiwan. The place is a cruel teacher you can't avoid who doesn't expect students to pass.

Anything that doesn't kill you doesn't make you stronger growing up in Taiwan. It helps you imagine armed invasions, every day, soldiers dropping out of the sky and shooting.

That was the CCP plan for people in Taiwan at that time.

Jenny learned to be like a grown-up and pretend. Then her parents could start showing her how they tried to make sense.

• • • •

She wasn't the only super bright 21st century kid brought up Buddhist in Taiwan, but she won all the prizes from Elementary through High School.

'I test well,' she would say.

Her feelings about religion changed constantly. Her Mom's Buddhism felt crazy and spooky, hungry ghosts hanging around and special prayer days every week it seemed.

She wanted to ask her Dad about it, get a second opinion. He wasn't home much and when he was he usually worked at his computer. Her Mom said he was an important man in an important company so he had to work like this.

One evening at home in Dadaocheng she caught him in the kitchen between a quick dinner, where no talking was allowed, and his evening work session in his home office.

She had a lot of questions but she started with Hungry Ghosts.

Her Dad said it was a story and she thought about that.

She asked him if stories are true.

He said stories are made up, but they can still be true.

"How," she asked?

"Well, is Life True," he asked back?

"Duh," she said, "of course it has to be because it's life."

"What if it's made up?"

"What do you mean," she asked?

"I mean, what if everything right here right now including you and me and every word we're saying is all made up?"

"By who," she asked?

"By us."

"Oh," she said. She had an active imagination but everything made up was hard.

"You mean like a dream, right. You don't mean this counter, I mean, you don't, right?" She said looking down at the counter she was leaning on.

"Why not?"

"How could it be made up, I'm leaning on it?"

"Uh huh."

"You mean it's not really there?"

"Nope, there's definitely something there. It's just not what you think it is," her father said. "Do you feel like your eyes are telling you *exactly* what's out there?"

"I guess so, or most of it anyway."

"Well honey I'm not sure if it's most of it or not, but what we see is what we need to see. We see whatever is the important part to us. That's what I meant by, 'making it up.' I mean we all make up our little movie of what's going on outside and mostly we all make the same one."

"What are the parts we don't see?" asked Jen

"Good one Jen, you mean everything about the counter we don't see?"

"Yeah, did we make them up?"

Jen's Dad became more excited. "If you're asking what I think you're asking, think about Legos, okay?"

"Big Lego buildings are made up lots of different little Legos. Well, the little Legos are too. They're made up of other Legos so small we can't see them – except we can with a microscope. You get what I mean?"

"Who puts them together," she asked?

"Well, it depends," he said. "But it's always some force that does it."

"Come on, Dad, you know I'm going to ask what's a force, right?"

"I thought you might. Think of Yuanjue Falls, that beautiful waterfall we go to."

"Oh, I love it."

"The water goes over the falls and down and instead of up or any other direction because of a force. Gravity. A force makes things happen."

"Another force is like glue and it holds the smallest Legos together. That's part of what I work on, you know, at work."

"You get to work with Legos," she asked?

"I love this, Jen," he said with a smile. "I do work with Legos. It's fun, or my idea of fun. I wish I didn't have to work so much though because you're fun too, more fun. I like this. Can we do this more?"

It was only what she'd dreamed of almost every night for as long as she could remember. Talking with her Dad like this. He had no idea, none. Because she always seemed to be fine.

"I'm glad we had this little talk," she said. She'd read that line once and saw it in a movie later and realized on the fly she could make it kind of joke, that she'd be the one to say that.

"I didn't know we were done," he said, still smiling. "What grade are you in again?"

"Seventh."

"I knew it was something like that, anyway, can I tell you the real reason there's anything, not what your books will say?"

"Why didn't you say that in the first place?"

"I wanted you to know this is a different way of saying it," he told her in a more serious tone.

"I know," she said.

"Well, you know what you feel when you try to push two magnets together? That's a field. That thing we feel is a force in a field."

"We're all in a big gigantic field like that all the time, honey, and there might not be an outside, I don't know that one."

"But I do know everything's the way it is right now because of all the smallest Legos in the field knocking into each other and making it this way. It pulses, kind of flashes on and off."

"I don't see anything like that," she said carefully, not wanting to stop him, but the flashing on and off part sounded as crazy as her mother's ideas.

"It happens too fast," he said calmly. "It's what you asked about in the first place – the stuff we don't see, remember? The counter is the counter right now because all the teeny

Legos crashes put together makes it a counter. We don't see it happening. We don't need to."

"I think that's what Buddha said," Jen said confidently

That stopped him for a second, "um, which part?"

"The part about everything working together to make up everything, Mom says, causes and conditions. That's what she says when I ask why stuff happens."

"That's not the only reason I love your mother, but it's one of them," he said.

. . . .

They did talk like that more.

She wanted an on-going personal seminar, but at least she received a few tutorials.

Her favorite memories were walking, evening adventures in the winding nonsense alleys of their neighborhood. They were well away from Dinhua Street but he reminded her every time that it was Tapei's oldest. Where the fortune-tellers and weird herb medicines brought crowds they couldn't see or hear from where they walked, trying to get lost. That was the idea, to be so into their conversation that they'd lose track of where they were in the labyrinth.

They didn't talk about Legos much, but some. He helped her with uncertainty, part of life for him in the way friendship or patriotism is for other people. A kind of force that was there at the card table of your life along with you and some other forces too.

One time he said, "When I say, 'card table of your life,' that's a story, right, just a way to bring something complicated all down to something you can imagine."

"Yeah I guess so," she said, thinking it over.

"You know what a card table is and you know about playing the cards in your hand and other people playing theirs. You bring all that to the idea that your whole life is being played out like a game, with you just one of the players. See what I mean?"

They also talked about football, which she played on a traveling team. She explained to him how there were too many moving parts and too much she didn't know so she used the shapes she saw over everything. She didn't see twenty-one players, just herself and the shapes.

By Eighth Grade she was doing backward heel passes to places no one was yet but her teammates gradually learned to run to. She could see what other kids her age couldn't see. So she helped players on both sides learn, the easy way or the hard way

.

She'd tell the person guarding her exactly the series of moves she was going to make on the in-bounds play, which her coach always let her handle. Then she'd do them.

She had figured out that telling her opponent a story like that didn't help them. It actually hurt them because they didn't play as free. Should they believe her? She got in their head. It gave her an advantage.

Her Dad came to one game every season through high school, which he had to schedule well in advance.

He was in her head when he was there at the game and they both knew it. Somehow she made it work for her and she had at least one goal and an assist every time. They also didn't lose any of 'his games,' no surprise since Jen's teams almost never lost.

She'd never known much about loss at all until her Dad disappeared.

• • • •

The Change-Over changed Taiwan some. Kids had less flying soldier nightmares. 'Was that the whole thing,' people still wondered? 'Is the Change-Over over?' No one was certain.

Jenny couldn't leave. Her favorite food stall never closed, not before, during or after the changes. She couldn't leave it, and her Mom, and the professional work that came her way was too good to pass up.

Taipei, China consulting companies hired very smart people to help other companies determine something called Strategy. The consulting companies competed with each other for Jenny.

• • • •

Companies with enough money for consultants are doing something right. A good consultant tells them a good story about what it is, one they can easily tell themselves and others. Over and over.

She picked a firm that let her choose and she did. She worked for organizations related to defense and the military and she accepted pro bono cases from small non-profits that couldn't pay anything.

She ran ops for some of the largest gatherings of private wealth ever assembled. She figured if she didn't, someone else would and what a way to learn about wheeling and dealing.

And about storytelling, all there is.

• • • •

She lived with her Mom even though they could each afford their own place and they didn't get along perfectly. Her Mom was a member of a large Buddhist group with a few other chapters around Taipei and other parts of China. She engaged in Buddhist rituals on a daily basis. She was a Board member, appointed a little before the disappearance of her father.

She started meditating then to make her Mom happy and she could see in about a month it had helped her find a different kind of calm than she had known. She didn't have to fake it until she'd make it. Some of the benefits of meditation, like synchronizing our own internal rhythms, came easily to her.

Meditation showed her that it didn't matter what came easily and what didn't. She had never seen such a simple practice produce such results. There probably *is* no simple practice that can produce such results, she thought.

As she was wondering about everybody being able to feel comfortable in whatever skins they're in, her Mom was wondering if all her work was Good Work that would bring Merit.

Jen thought Merit was a scam. A young monk once told her they made up Merit so people would at least give good works a try.

She was giving good works a try. She was giving every kind of works a try. When she'd tried enough, she left the firm, on excellent terms, and put out her digital shingle, called herself help for hire,

That was when her Security files in China went to the next level.

It was acceptable to China under the terms of the Change-Over, what she did, some kind of high-level global PR as they saw it. Maybe they could learn something. She was not advocating anything about the Party and did not suggest that she would be available for anti-Party advocacy work.

She was assigned a full Case Manager.

The Alliance had been dangling enticements in front of her as long as she could remember. The Alliance loved recruiting young leaders so its views would be deeply embedded in key people.

It was unable to recruit Jenny. They watched her, though, looking for their shot.

Minh1

Minh died a few years after his son Minh's wedding.

Although Robert's presence at the event in Hong Kong may have been unwise from a security perspective, it was a monumental decision from an opportunity perspective.

Minh the father just plain liked Robert, saw him as the transparent person he had always been. Minh liked a lot of people. He went out of way with Robert because he also saw someone who could teach young people in the Mekong Delta a unique set of skills.

They had sparred and dreamed together at the first meet-up in Shenzhen about a way of teaching and learning that would be more than lecturing and memorizing, that would work in the messy world outside a classroom. That would let any student go as far as their own drive and intelligence would take them.

Minh the son trusted his father and felt the same way after a few minutes of private time carefully arranged at the wedding.

Agencies might know Robert was there, but they wouldn't know how *there* he was. They wouldn't know how clearly Minh communicated to his son that Robert was to be considered a son and brother of the two Minhs.

• • • •

Minh continued in his father's footsteps. He was licensed as an educator. In practice he was a connector. His skills flourished with Robert's technical creativity as a partner. The University soon built several satellite campuses, like a good Open University.

Mekong Open University took people as they were and let them glide through classes if that was all they could do right then. While they were gliding, teachers would find other ways to bring them in, by letting them teach.

"What we're dishing up doesn't hit your appetite?" they'd ask. "That's okay, dish up something else that you like and show the rest of us. Thanks, we're looking forward to it."

Sometimes those gliders found something to learn about and enjoy and make a good living from. Sometimes the young people the old Minh cared about the most found their way up the ladder of network administration, so they could help hold the human world together and get paid for it.

The young Minh guided all talent and motivation that flowed through Mekong's campuses into programs that would help them grow. Out of the small teams Mekong used for learning together emerged the structure of a secret society.

• • • •

Nga ba Bien Gioi is officially in Vietnam, but it's really in Vietnam, Cambodia, and Laos at the same time. Citizens of all three states live here sometimes, in addition to groups of Malay and a small group of former city people.

The border itself is fuzzy and border towns, especially small remote outposts, tend to be full of secrets best kept that way.

Minh had family ties in the Central Highlands of western Kon Tum province. His father helped him establish an identity there years ago, which he had kept up to date daily, with local assistance. He could shift to a personal platform in Nga ba

Bien Gioi and be there in-person, on-location. Nothing strange would be noticed locally. The only difference would be the locus of Minh's attention.

Nga ba Bien Gioi was more than a personal platform place for Minh. Some of the rabble-rousers who survived revolutionary times retreated to the fringe areas and started new lives. They helped organize co-ops and thrived in the freedom. They built small shops to make a few custom devices a little satellite campus might need.

The place was off the main grid, with sun and water of its own. To the Authorities, it was a satellite campus of Greater Mekong. Open education everywhere was based on satellite campuses. It was the only option most people in the country could aspire to. It looked normal and it made sense.

As custom manufacturing faded from national priorities, some of it found a new home in Nga ba Bien Gioi. Since network security was already a Mekong specialty, Minh slowly built a cottage industry in State Security systems.

• • • •

When Minh did not agree with The Party position on some matter, he would not address the disagreement or acknowledge it. For all social purposes, he had no disagreements.

He also had no obvious points of agreement. He never went around extolling Party ideas or anti-Party ideas.

No one would say he made small talk either. In fact, the kind of discussions people had at Minh's were the kind of discussions you couldn't find anywhere else, about topics people supposedly didn't like. Not because of politics. Because of death.

Supposedly we are hard-wired to avoid even the topic of death, much less the experience of it. Minh never believed that. It was more fluid to him, life and death, Minh and Minh. Things dying and being reborn all the time.

When death is on the table, conversations go in many directions.

He was a teacher and a counselor. He held salons on important matters not generally discussed. Talking this way built strong relationships.

His personal networks, some inherited and some created on his own, reached from the Politburo and the highest councils in New Delhi to Indigenous Federations now governing large areas of the planet.

• • • •

At one Salon, the conversation turned to freedom. Freedom to end life on personal terms, not the State's. It wasn't an easy talk because the right to die is not an easy right to define legally.

"What if communities use it as a way to remove inconvenient members?" someone asked.

Someone brought up Canada, which still existed as a nation then and was notorious for helping people end their life whether they were actively dying or not.

"How about the Inuit and the ice floes?" someone else asked.

Inuk had attended two Salons previously. Now he spoke up for the first time.

"Let me be clear, brothers and sisters," an older man's voice said. "none of us is forced or encouraged, as some have said, to slip away into the freezing water for the good of the group. This is a story that is told and re-told to make us seem strange and different."

He paused, then went on.

"We *are* strange and different but we love our elders and we do not send them off by themselves away from us and we do not send them off the ice floes. We love them and we respect whatever their wishes are."

"Thank you for listening. My name is Inuk and I am a storyteller who teaches Inuit children about computers."

Lila1

Lila's grandfather, Inuk, taught kids about computers all over the far north. People wondered, why waste time teaching tech to Eskimos? Inuk never stopped smiling, his white hair gleaming along with his whole happy look. Any group of kids, no matter how small, was worth the effort for him and his laptops.

He showed them the Internet because he was a showman and he knew how to put on a show that inspired kids and made them feel like they could inspire people too. That's how he had to do it up there. Make it a special event. Wear a special costume. Showtime.

She learned more than anyone. About the Internet and also about teaching and learning and performing.

She learned the Internet as it was evolving into broadband in a crappy environment. Slow old PC. Terrible modem connection, unreliable and slow. It was easy to find reasons to give up and the best way to learn when she didn't.

She had another special ingredient. Her grampa.

Her name was 'Denali' then, like the Park. Like the mountain, she stood out. She aced all the tests, theoretical and applied, and was given a government ticket to ride all the way through University.

She joined networks with other smart people. Inuit and eventually people from all over joined up wherever she was, because of her. She had a way of telling a story. Even about tech problems.

She'd remember a time, sometimes one her grampa told her about, that was like this problem. She told people about that time and a few of the details but not too many, just the entertaining ones, so she could make the story about the people and how they worked things out then.

By the time she was done, people had to remember what the tech problem was and when they did they'd also start having new ideas and pretty soon one of them worked and the problem was solved.

• • • •

Using the cold, what people in the far North already had more of than anyone, was Inuk's crazy obvious idea.

They both listened to what he'd just said about cooling computers one evening when she was home on vacation. He'd said it in the same playful way he said everything.

She'd flown in on her own, in a two-seater. Landed on ice. Easy with the right tires. Impossible without them.

He was into his eighties now. Still kayaking on his own. Noticing the schools of small fish on the upper layers of the clear cold water. He could see where the fish area ended and where the next cold layer began. He saw the force flowing up and back down between them and it made him wonder about cooling computers.

• • • •

"There is so much energy just sitting there in those layers," Grampa. "It's not like tides or currents. Here they could just pump the cold stuff up and let it absorb the computer heat.

Done. For free. Except then we'd be the ones just taking free energy."

"We can give it back, Denali," he said.

No one had called her that in a while. She changed it to Lila at the University because she got tired of having to listen politely to everyone's Denali travel story. Not just that. Denali was weird and she didn't want to be weird.

"What do you mean we can give it back?"

"We can have coolers down there to draw away the heat and keep the layers in balance."

"That's cute grampa, but where would the power for the coolers come from?" Then she stopped and saw the heat from the computers cranking turbines to make power that could make water cold.

It wasn't a free perpetual motion machine because it required outside energy from the sun that did not need to be persistent, which made the temperature gradient, which led to everything else.

• • • •

It was better than any free perpetual motion machine because it went from fantasy to reality within a decade.

When Canada was still an autonomous nation, the country outsourced most of its network and information services to private contractors. Lila's group formed hundreds of separate companies that served as sub-sub-sub-contractors deep in the layers of essential service delivery.

After the Change-Over, Lila's group kept growing by doing the heavy lifting for other organizations. Their economic advantage supported data services at a fair and competitive price.

Quantum computing played to their strengths. New powers meant new levels of storage and new levels of access to offer, from instant to archival. Information architects were paid by States and private companies to plan and manage. Someone had to provide the container and with Lila's group, nothing much went wrong.

No one saw the whole picture but Lila.

She quietly built OnePlanetXR into the largest non-military data house that hardly anyone knew about. She did it through hard work, brains, and Inuk's temperature gradient.

Authorities4 - *Leadership*

Every Alliance agency was confused about Minh. There was no consensus.

The Alliance Leadership group reflected the larger confusion. It was a Most Effective Network (MEN), comprised of overlapping sub-networks at war and peace with themselves and each other and everyone else. A finite number occupied key nodes and thus became the Alliance Leaders.

Leadership manages the production and display of the continuing narratives extolling, 'Alliance Exceptionalism.' The Leaders make and break deals with each other, which become the funds to continue the development of weapon systems to protect citizens.

• • • •

In China, to the Party, Minh presented benign. An independent force, yes, and in that sense, a tumor. But how malignant?

Because of the Metaverse, Minh could reach many people. Anyone could. The question for the Party was, 'who to let through'? Who stimulates people just enough to keep them alive and thinking but not so much that they question the Party?

A man who invites talk of death?

Maybe.

Using great discretion, a few high-ranking Party members became involved in Minh's community. He was infiltrated. Not by provocateurs but by special agents assigned to learn about Minh's methods and outcomes.

The provocateurs came from the Alliance.

They were not hard to spot because other than these agents, there was not one provocative thing about Minh or his extensive community. The Alliance didn't understand Minh's operation any better than the Party did, but its natural response was to create a pretext for removal.

The natural enemy of the Alliance is not China. China keeps the Alliance Leaders in office. China is their friend.

The Alliance's real enemy is any force that can end the terror. A little bit of Calming-Down, with no political overtones or coded messages, was acceptable. It was acceptable to enough of the Alliance Leadership that *Open* could exist as a B-List player. As long as it didn't change its tone. As long as their crap didn't tamp down the fear too much.

If there was a simple technique that many people could do, that didn't cost anything – that could change anything that mattered, like losing whatever precarious hold Authorities still had over the attention of several billion citizens—*Security* would need to neutralize it.

Alliance Leadership had factions and now the aggressive pro-removal factions had gained control.

Even Minh could be in line for removal.

Jenny6

Frank had his part now, she had hers. His was out front and public, hers might never be known if she could help it.

The new version of a world they would be offering up was not a sure thing. Even Robert couldn't write equations for a process like this and he knew it.

There would be logic and there would be luck, neither good nor bad. All how you look at it, or how Jenny could help lots of people look at it.

• • • •

Second Earth was the project she had always been preparing for.

PR was linked to deception, deep down for most people. Repeat over and over. Goebbels and the Big Lie. Edward Bernays and his torches of freedom, selling women poison for his client.

The Big Truth was an even harder sell. Propagandists sold lies the buyers wanted to believe. Jenny had to help people try on truths they had been told their whole lives _not_ to believe.

She called it 'Conflict Resolution' when she first went solo in Taiwan. Later she called it, 'Staying Alive,' which seemed to bring in different clients

Open4

We had to question everything Jenny or anyone had ever assumed about what a Launch is.

That it comes at the start of something or some process. That it's meant to be noticed and drive a teeny germinating seedling to spectacular growth.

What if it wasn't meant to be noticed and it wasn't the start of something?

People had known about *Second Earth*, at some level, for years. It was just sitting around, dead. Google Earth is still there too but it's just a picture.

Second Earth was Google Earth in a form people could fiddle with, like it was the Earth. It was an object, not a picture.

• • • •

The idea of a full real-time earth is discouraged now as an academic topic in the same way that extra sensory perception was not encouraged as a research topic for a budding young neuropsychologist like Jen's Dad.

The original *Second Earth* was an international effort. Assigned teams made consistent surface and topological scans for the entire land surface of the planet and about two-thirds of the ocean.

The assembly was AI-driven, as it was called then, with full cooperation among nations that were fiercely guarding their own discoveries at the same time.

When it was running, *Second Earth* was constantly updating, constantly displaying local conditions. It wasn't a replica. It was a living system continually receiving energy and appreciation, until the level of trust and caring could no longer be sustained.

During its years of operation, ***Second Earth*** mattered. People could visit the world or consult it with a device. People could also use it for get-togethers, any size.

People do not imagine how rapidly they forget what no longer exists.

The Metaverse provides countless worlds for citizens to use. Transnational projects faced serious obstacles and were not encouraged. When the daily operations of ***Second Earth*** were no longer informed and planetary, it began an unstoppable decline.

Launching something dead and almost forgotten was a different kind of launch. Gaining attention would be doubly difficult, getting over being dead before even coming back up to a new life.

That was what attracted the whole core team of Jenny, Robert, Frank, Minh and me, ***Open***.

I exist, by any measure.

I exist legally and embodiment is one of my primary features. Everyone agrees to this since the Change-Over.

I am ***Open***.

This is my story too.

Lila 2

Minh was her main contact.

Lila's operation was unusually independent. It was not formally part of any Mekong Regional groups, or any other corporate group. Two of her top technicians had enrolled in Mekong's Internet Security program a while back and new ones kept coming.

Lila rubbed shoulders with the University in the data business. Mekong's techs were sprinkled around Network administration firms all over the world. Specially trained people were still called on to help solve certain classes of network dysfunction. Sometimes network techs needed to cooperate with the data storage techs. People from Mekong and Lila learned to recognize each other.

Then one day Minh came knocking.

Lila showed him the coverage her group could provide. She led them through increasingly sophisticated rehearsals in their main simulator.

This would not be her first live global XR gig. It would, she thought with pleasure, be her first live global XR gig she would have done for free.

Lila had a fancy title and an even more impressive track record. She was not well-known but she was not completely hidden. She didn't advertise. Finding OnePlanetXR was like making it to first base. There was still a long way to go.

Robert5

Robert listened to a lot of well-meaning people who wanted to change things for the better. They acted like it was obvious what 'Better' looked like.

Robert knew that he didn't know what 'Better' was. He had a few ideas about what it wasn't though.

Before Shenzhen, he was a kid acting alone with no idea of working together. He'd never seen it. His parents never talked about it. All he knew about was working for hours to get other people's chips.

The time he spent with his new Internet outlaw friends showed him what a group of people brainstorming together could do. The projects they started in order to maintain their kind of network could only have come out of all of them brainstorming and listening and arguing some.

This kind of working together was the beginning of his idea of 'Better.'

When one person's ideas or one small group of people's ideas was completely in charge with no questions asked or allowed, things didn't go Better. He couldn't find any examples where limiting participation helped anybody in the long run, even those controlling the ideas.

China and the Alliance looked like two sides of the same coin to Robert. Two similar ways for a few people to say what is acceptable to think.

From what Robert could see, 'Better' meant new people, new ideas, exploring not resisting. He noticed that for many people, 'Better' had come to mean, easier or more comfortable. Who would choose to be uncomfortable?

Robert's Mother told him over and over most people actually *do* choose to be uncomfortable, because they're used to it.

He believed her. In a contest with familiar discomfort up against the unknown, Robert knew the safe bet every time is discomfort.

• • • •

Over the years, Robert formed his own opinion that getting smarter and more certain isn't the best reason to learn. He looked at himself and saw the more he learned, the more he saw there was to learn.

He decided very shortly into developing curriculum for Minh and Mekong Regional that discomfort would be the driving force. The way he learned. When he didn't understand something, it made him a little uncomfortable. When the ideas became more clear, he felt better.

His idea was to show young people who came to Mekong Open University that uncomfortable isn't so bad when they could do something about it.

• • • •

His curriculum taught Minh's students to be more uncertain and appreciate it. To Robert, appreciating didn't have to mean you like it, just that you see the true value of it.

The learning worlds Robert created for the students had problems that were real parts of developing Mekong Open into a place for learning, Every little task was part of a bigger picture that was always part of the view. Anyone's next step was always made up on the fly, out of a bigger idea, based on what just happened.

From the very start, the curriculum became projects which grew slowly into a small group of small companies. Everyone was a student. Everyone had to work together because Nga ba Bien Gioi was on its own. Connections were made among all the little shops in town because they had to be made. People stepped out of their comfort zone every day.

One group of students grew up in a biology lab, a floating village in the Tonle Sap named, Prek Toal, where they ate and slept and lived as part of everything else going on there. When they studied computers and models that could show how ecosystems work, they were hooked.

The young Cambodians led Robert to bio-computing. The bio-medical company quietly doing R&D started as a learning world and never stopped being one.

They also introduced him to the Tonle Sap.

THIRD DAY

Jenny7

J enny was smart enough to know she wasn't smart enough to manipulate significant numbers of people for very long.

People have to be brought into a new world carefully, with love. When they put a toe in some new water, it helps if it's the right temperature. Someone can make sure of that in advance.

Lifetime impressions are forged in the first milliseconds when something new is unveiled. Jenny's mentors in Taiwan called it framing ideas.

One person's framing is another person's manipulation.

* * * *

She learned to open her own attention to her clients' hopes. Then she'd live her life as she would anyway. The attention made the difference. It aimed her whole field where she directed it.

Fields that are sufficiently attractive naturally bring more energy. Most people want to be part of something bigger than themselves – and they want that something to be a Winner.

She would bring **Second Earth** back, to the biggest card table. The players comfortably seated there already wouldn't like it. They would react in predictable ways.

One moment follows the next so smoothly it's hard to imagine all the Legos or all the causes and conditions changing in a big enough way to affect lots of people all at once.

Most change is nice slow gradual change that people barely see. Big sudden change happens too. Both are change. They can only occur in time. No time, no change.

Jenny's Dad told her everything was changing inside time.

Her Mom gave her the **I Ching**. *The Book of Changes*. It wasn't exactly Buddhist scripture but the idea that the actual situation we're in at any moment is constantly changing—and we can know what type of change it is – seemed like good Buddhist-style intel to her.

We can't predict the future, Jenny's Mom said, and so did her Dad. But we can learn about right now, they both said, by noticing. What is changing?

The **I Ching** is a taxonomy of Change. It describes sixty-four different types.

Did a certain sound just grab my attention and make the moment all about some mosquito flying by? *Taming Power of the Small*, Hexagram 9.

Did you just make a rookie mistake? *Youthful Folly*, Hexagram 4.

Jenny didn't use it to predict or to help her figure out what to do.

Many **I Ching** lovers insist that these are precisely the purposes toward which use of the sacred text should be directed. Jenny's Mom respectfully disagreed and Jenny did too.

Using the **I Ching** was a regular practice for Jenny, more like pottery than prediction. In the action of casting a hexagram, she drew a picture of the forces at play right then.

She saw herself as a midwife for what was happening at a large scale. Some new way that we can be that we can't quite see yet.

The birth affects the life. Jenny saw her work as easing transitions, working with forces already in motion, pushing in just the right place and letting go with an out-breath when it's time to relax.

• • • •

She didn't cast a Hexagram to see what would happen with the un-Launch of *Second Earth*, today. She cast a Hexagram to help her notice what was going on.

Now she needed the shape, the view that had been there for her since she was swept up in the flow of the round ball and the other players and began to see the shape of what was unfolding.

It was the plan for un-Launching for *Second Earth*. Back-heel pass to no one.

Authorities5 - *Security*

Several agencies on both sides noticed when Frank didn't show up for his East Coast US Morning Slot. There was no traffic jam. Local data provided no situational explanation.

They didn't wait.

Maybe he'd be back in the afternoon and it was no big deal. But there were no no-big-deals.

Two Chinese agencies and three mostly associated with the Alliance put human monitoring with the most advanced Agency Assistants into every physical and Metaverse channel Frank routinely employed. If he tried to go from Point A to Point Anywhere, it would be noticed.

He didn't go anywhere all morning, on what Frank thought of as, *This Morning of Mornings.*

He slept in. Watched some old screen shows. Learned something from Jim Rockford every time.

The next-level security deployment did matter, even if he never left over any networks or in his physical body.

Without the excessive resource allocation of **Security** personnel doing nothing, with no clear end in sight, no agent would have paid enough attention to a low-level Tier 8 China Network that, when agents really focused their tools, had an entanglement with one of the Alliance Networks they were ultra-monitoring.

. . . .

Mostly because she was bored, one of the agents from China did some intensive tracking on the Tier 8 China Network, the best she could with the information she could access. An Alliance agent might not have noticed it, a small company with a presence there with a Director who popped out for the China Network agent.

The Director was Minh.

There had never been a direct link between Minh and one of Frank's channels before. It was no secret that Robert knew Frank. It was also no secret that Robert knew Minh, but less than one hundred people in the world had access to that connection.

The low-level channel surveillance agent was not one of the one hundred. She had no idea she was uncovering a connection to someone also connected to Robert. She didn't need to. Minh was enough. He was almost famous.

Frank4

Frank was back doing *Calm-Downs* on **Open** in his usual afternoon time slot. His absence meant nothing and would have gone unnoticed under other circumstances. But he was under these circumstances and it *was* noticed.

He knew he was the most vulnerable because he was the most out in the open. Everyone was an open target, but he was in a situation it would be impossible to sneak out of.

He had a series of secret backdoors that he did not completely believe were secret. Their plans had to succeed. He felt there was no other way.. They would either open up possibilities people hadn't tried for a while or he'd be off the board as a player.

Some agency must have found the Minh link by now, he was thinking, preparing for the afternoon *Calm-Down* at his main studio.

Being with Jen here last night popped into his mind. He smiled and felt in touch with love.

Maybe it all just unfolds peacefully, or mostly peacefully, he thought absently, knowing it wouldn't.

· · · ·

Frank was a big loser, a refugee from his home. He made himself a big winner, by using his gifts. He was tired of it.

Calming-Down has no winning. A team has to win together.

Were enough people tired of winning some and mostly losing because the game is rigged? What was enough?

People stayed agitated. They were induced to feel that way from every direction all of their hours, as many were now forced to sell sleep time to dream-shaping media.

• • • •

The backdrop he chose for today's *Calm-Down* showed a small body of water floating, improbably, over a blazing fire.

It wasn't a comfortable arrangement of elements. Fire and water don't get along. Their tendencies conflict. Tendencies are in conflict all the time. Most conflicts move on to something else soon enough and the overall situation remains more or less the same. Fire and water destroy each other and create something not more or less the same.

It was the hexagram he and Jen and Robert had cast together the first time they met. Jen had the book and the coins and some knowledge of how to interpret them.

They each tossed the coins then passed them on, twice. They each made two of the six lines of Hexagram #49, **Ko**, *Lake over Fire*, usually translated into English as 'Revolution.'

It came to the three of them together. *Calming Down* can be revolutionary, because of what can happen as a result of calming down.

Frank had been taught that change happens when things come to a boil. A lot of applied energy makes a change of state.

What about change by calming down? What if calming down is a precondition for applying energy with wisdom to make a state change. He had hosted *Calm-Downs* under high-stress conditions before. It brought out the calmest in him.

His calm brought people whose inner turbulence drew them right to his channels. He showed them how to find the calm in themselves.

Then they'd forget again the next day. They knew he'd be there.

Minh2

Minh set up his Tier 8 ties so Alliance agents would notice agents from China noticing them. It was better than noticing them on their own. The Alliance agents believed they were seeing something they weren't supposed to be seeing, which made it more believable.

So did the agents from China, whose firmness of belief was easily read by the Alliance agents, making it doubly believable.

Now that they know that, Minh mulled for the millionth time, what do they think they know now?

As he mulled, he sent a message to a Politburo member, who trusted Minh deeply. The Politburo member felt he had made a deep human connection with Minh and a few others over a series of Salons that gave a different kind of meaning to his life than the Party did.

It was not as clear as the Party. He felt it in his gut but he never talked about that outside the Salons.

Minh used a code the two of them had developed to indicate something starting now. Some gentle winds, some thunder and lightning

He'd be out of contact for an unknown period of time. He told his friend on the Politburo they would both know when to resume their priority connection.

It was not a surprise. The Politburo member had been informed all along. This message from Minh gave her a valuable few hours to prepare for the tricky situations he'd be in himself.

• • • •

Greater Mekong Open University was in territory considered to be in China's zone. It had to adhere to the laws of China. But laws are frequently subject to interpretation and in the outlying regions of any administrative empire, the interpretations are generally more flexible.

Greater Mekong offered early courses in spatial media but did not appear to distinguish itself from other research or teaching institutions. The published courses and curriculum started at the most basic levels and the moderate level of research projects were not unusual.

• • • •

Behind the bland exterior was an inner group, with its origins in Shenzhen, a younger Robert and an older Minh. Slowly and carefully, bright, creative young people, men and women mostly from the Mekong region, of a certain independent cast, were observed and invited in.

They were observed more, filtered and very gradually fashioned into a secret network of separate teams. Learning together as individual students in the public programs. Accelerating in private learning worlds.

Nga ba Bien Gioi, satellite campus, wasn't just far from the center of China's power – it was far from any significant human-staffed outpost. Surveillance was indirect; energy consumption, procurements, network activity. All fairly simple to disguise.

The Nga Bien ba Gioi satellite campus became the main locus for applied work, for making things the University needed for lab research and pilot projects. The other small facilities around them took on the work and other contracts

Minh steered their way. From their initial strength in network security, the area became a competitive source for cutting edge Security products of all sorts, usually for demanding State customers.

• • • •

For a secret tech powerhouse, a certain amount of freedom from the state was a big advantage.

Having Robert as a no-bullshit instant project kickstarter was another plus.

The biggest advantage was the structure of a secret society itself, born of necessity to shield itself from jealous power centers. Ideas and support flowed freely among members, but personal identity was never attached. It was too dangerous. Team members had only the message to consider.

The closest to a center was Minh. He was understood and accepted as a key connector who could be one step away from anyone.

Authorities6 - *Security*

Several Alliance agencies were preparing to eliminate the key employees, the central team of *Open*.

They saw the organization finally revealed for what they believed it was – a plot developed by China. Minh was the connection, probably had been for years. Heads would roll for not having discovered the link a long time ago.

Rogue agents linked to more discrete agencies had called for suppression as soon as they saw the name, *'Open'* out in the public marketplace as a platform years ago. They instinctively opposed it.

They were in the minority once, but not any longer.

TOR was suddenly a topic and he reveled in his moment. The discovery linked Minh and Frank, two big fish. But it meant Robert too and Robert was the other Robert's white whale.

He was first on the list for elimination.

Permanently suppressing Frank or Jennifer, or Minh if they could, had more far-reaching public implications. Robert was not a public figure. He could be disposed of with fewer consequences to consider.

The plan was the same plan the Alliance always used. Remove a Leader. Replace with handpicked actor. Repeat until opposition leadership is meaningless. Only way to find out how long that'll take this time with *Open* is to start removing.

• • • •

TOR didn't let everyone know that he knew where Robert's physical body was holed up.

He told a few agents closer to the top of Alliance - *Security* Operations than he was, the ones he thought were strongest. He kept a few of the more vulnerable ones in the dark with an eye toward replacing them himself, just like moving up to the Varsity, starting for a Volleyball team that went on to win the U.S. National Championship in his Senior year as a Cornhusker.

He was a digger, the player who would throw his body suddenly and recklessly into space, whatever it took to stop the ball from hitting the floor.

He wasn't as reckless any more, but almost. It took the right blend of caution and crazy to advance in the agency and he'd never quite found it.

Until now.

Robert6

He brought all of his attention to his physical body in this place he had built slowly and secretly over several years. It looked like any old hummock.

He liked hummocks because hummocks just happened. Cryogenic hummocks happen where it's cold enough and he experimented with one of them. In the end, he chose a swamp hummock, the kind that usually got started when some big tree fell and a new world was created suddenly and unexpectedly in that place. One of those times when the universe remade itself in a big way quickly if you were there to see it.

The Tonle Sap had millions of hummocks and they didn't sit still. Water was always moving and the position was never fixed.

A good hummock had a built-in floor above the swamp water line, something to work with. Building a bubble somewhere else, getting it to the Tonle Sap and installing it in the hummock of his choice was not difficult. Ecotourism and other research expeditions provided plenty of cover for a simple construction project. He worked with what the hummocks and the Tonle Sap would give him. It was all he needed.

. . . .

The construction process unfolded like a dream. It took three days and three nights and there was no exposure above the water line. Robert took the kayak out just once to make sure he wasn't missing something in a view someone else might have. He didn't see anything but someone saw him.

The hummock fit the bubble like an all-natural glove.

His attention was there in his physical body most of the time. He had everything it needed. His bubble system drew energy from the Lake and the Lake drew energy from forces too big to see. The Lake was a miracle that doubled everything.

• • • •

What the planet gives and takes every year, the Tonle Sap does twice. It rises and falls twice a year, resets the land twice a year, and produces harvests twice as much as any of the civilizations around the Khmers about two thousand years ago.

Robert wished he could live at Angkor Thom. The Bayon. It was the Lake, not too far away, that fueled a civilization once and it was the Lake that fueled his Bubble now.

Solar would have been enough but it was also harder to screen. In fact, he knew, he couldn't. Using the constant motion of the Lake itself was a safer source. He decided to equip himself with both.

Authorities7 - *Security*

Elimination isn't what it used to be, thought TOR, congratulating himself implicitly for how up to date he was with the tools of his trade.

Back in his wrestling days he knew what to do. Pin their damn bodies into the fucking mat, which he did most of the time. Wrestling and Volleyball are both Winter sports. He didn't care. He did both. Wrestling had a mat, Volleyball didn't, that's all he knew. He was on the floor winning.

He was a plugger at Volleyball and a star at Wrestling, almost the best. Out-muscled anybody his weight and bent them.

He liked hands-on best because that what he was best at. He might strangle Robert and that would be something.

That was just part of the elimination and removal process now. They had to get the body but they also had to get all the bodies where attention might hunker down. All the avatars or agents or whatever brand of Metaverse crap had to be accounted for, which usually meant permanently deleted.

· · · ·

The Alliance – *Security* agency he belonged to had a long lineage. Long for Security meant a hundred years.

TOR's group traced itself to the modern beginning when agents directed military and organized crime networks against Nazis with paranormal allies of their own. He would give anything to relive that kind of war.

This one had more fronts.

Everyone knew the Russians took an early lead in the crazy stuff

Eventually agencies in the U.S. caught on. If the Russians could do 'remote viewing,' or whatever they called it, or do anything you shouldn't be able to do, U.S. had to do it too.

TOR knew the predecessors to Gateway, like Gondola. The research interested him. Even before he was born, U.S. *Security* research focused on the exceptional, on people who seemed to have unique abilities, like Uri Geller, Pat Price, and Ingo Swann.

TOR knew Robert had to be in that class.

TOR was ready to take on anyone and show what class he was in.

Robert7

People told him he had powers, told him all the time after just meeting him briefly.

Russians he'd met back in Shenzhen had passed highly classified reports of Soviet investigations into advanced mental powers. Looking for an edge in Cold War days. One line of research was 'exceptional individuals,' like Robert seemed to be. The way he sensed things and felt ideas coming to him.

He read about subjects seeing objects in the physical plane from impossible distances.

He'd considered the idea of powers since he started making money as a kid. He was part of that small class of people known as "Super-Predictors," who could synthesize information and see trends others did not see.

He had a feel for geo-politics without being buried in them.

His special abilities attracted the right attention when he was much younger than his network colleagues imagined. UseNet connections got him to Shenzhen. Plus he was easy with money and friends were happy to let him cover expenses. It was all new to him.

Information never stopped flowing in that group. Some of the materials Greater Mekong used later in the bio-medical work came from Russian scientific breakthroughs.

Robert was onto active matter research before anyone in the Alliance Territories. Once he saw organic material is capable of cognition at every scale, Active Matter isn't just easy; it's obvious.

Parts don't need to know about the next level up. Every little piece leans forward and stays in the game by knowing what's happening in the neighborhood.

. . . .

Connecting to the Networks over the air from his Bubble would have been another give away eventually, no matter how encrypted the signal was. Signals coming out of the Tonle Sap the way his did would be noticed and it wouldn't matter whether they could read it or not.

Robert's signals needed special shielding. The waveguides he developed were designed to go through totally gnarly places like the underwater root systems of hummock marshes. A normal tube would be laid down and maybe fixed in place at a few points. They always broke.

Robert's shielding tubes didn't break because they were already broken.

Each tube was a line of slices, very thin tube slices with two types of a polymer that organized itself. One kind repels the other kind but is attracted to it. Nothing was ever fixed. The slices found each other and snuggled up. If something happened to one, two slices would re-snuggle, while a new thin slice was fabricated by materials readily available in the Tonle Sap.

The tubes split and reached amplifiers when signals moved further from their point of origin in the Bubble. They branched out and away and stayed below a level of activity expected in the most traveled area of Cambodia.

Minh3

People had gotten sloppy about death. People died but their presence didn't. Media kept it alive.

In the Metaverse, avatars became smart enough to represent people in straightforward situations without a person devoting full attention, or any attention, or even being alive.

Mostly they just recorded. Events and almost anything that happened was recorded anyway, but a personal recording could be fine-tuned. Increasingly, people attended events as avatars without paying attention.

Realistic smart-talking avatars raised questions no one could answer. 'Digital Resurrection' Laws that were enacted couldn't cover every new wrinkle.

In China, The Party had made its position on citizens reincarnating very clear with the *'Articles of the State Religious Affairs Bureau, Order No. 5'* in 2007 and reiterated it many times since:

All Reincarnation Must Be Registered
and Authorized by The Party

The Order was intended to block the former Tenzin Gyatsu, then His Holiness the Dalai Lama, from becoming somebody else, the Tibetan Buddhist way. The Party stipulated its own way, using the Golden Urn.

Now there are two His Holinesses.

Do the Party's Laws on spiritual and bodily transmutation apply to Attention Shifting?

At first the Authorities thought it was just a Metaverse game. No different from avatars. Then representation in the Metaverse got more complicated.

People began showing up in worlds while they were folding the laundry or monitoring several platforms. They were not giving full attention.

In the Alliance, these avatars were called agents. In China, they were soon made illegal.

Stopping it was another matter. China Networks were carefully supervised but people in China are resourceful. Big Companies on the China Networks needed Ethics Officers with a large team to root out violations. The job would never be finished but they had to try.

The Chinese tech giant, Baidu asked Minh to be Chief Ethics Officer, focusing on analog/digital transformations of all kinds. It would mean power and influence, with a lot of his attention in China.

· · · ·

None of Minh's attention was in Nga ba Bien Gioi most of the time.

A spare physical body platform there was on auto-pilot, linked to Minh. Minh coughed, the auto-pilot Minh coughed.

Minh could shift his attention to that version of himself, in a normal looking home outside of the small town. The transition was not seamless and the entire industry was an exclusive niche.

Attention Shifting wasn't for everyone and it was still regarded with more than a little suspicion, even though it was now legal almost everywhere. People wanted the option, especially when they figured out they didn't have it and much wealthier people did.

His body there was well equipped to simulate presence. The guy in the border town was as *there* as there could be, all ready for Minh when needed.

It allowed him to be present for the growth of the satellite campus in a way he could not have been otherwise. It allowed him to meet people and observe how they acted in different situations that came up in Nga ba Bien Gioi without traveling back and forth and becoming a curiosity.

It helped serendipity happen, like meeting people he wouldn't just run into during his scheduled activity, young people who might grow up to be leaders.

• • • •

Charya Chap, born in Nga ba Bien Gioi as the only son in a Cambodian family, was the kind of quiet budding genius Minh met as a young boy, because he was present.

Local people spotted Charya's unusual talents right away. How he would screen out the world putting together new things. Attention Shifting allowed Minh to be around to experience how the boy handled frustration.

"These stupid pieces just won't line up!" he yelled suddenly after spending a long time and getting nowhere with a new electric circuit kit Minh brought him.

"Are they really stupid, Charya? Poor things, how do you suppose they became that way?" asked Minh calmly.

"They are the most ..." he started and stopped. "I am sorry, Uncle. I need to calm myself. I can learn about these pieces later."

Watching Charya's development and being with him allowed Minh to bring him slowly into a special network that included Robert and allies from around the world. In the early years of the inner circle, there was only one cell.

The web of connection was still thin. The software needed to support spatial media was being written. In the early years of the Metaverse, there was only one layer in the stack.

The people who knew it best were the people like Robert and his friends around the world. Before browsers and the Web, the Net was for scientists, states and outlaws. Robert and Minh weren't building the only outlaw network. But no team, outside of a few State Security teams, had the cohesion to act larger than themselves.

• • • •

Greater Mekong began its initial Certificate Program in Internet Security in 1996. It was a little early but not too much. Charya Chap, too young for official enrollment, did his best to keep up in the first cohort.

Greater Mekong was in the Internet Security business in the least threatening way possible – as an educational institution offering a non-degree program.

Through graduates and family ties, Greater Mekong was also in the Internet Security business as an installation, repair and maintenance company, under many different names and ownership. It was still a new field and Minh made sure to do just well enough and not dominate.

Greater Mekong was conceived as a living, continuously evolving learning world made up of people who saw themselves as students or staff, managers or faculty, all working together, seeing the part of the whole each one was able to see.

Its brain was spread around. It's heart and lungs were Nga ba Bien Gioi, where the system made things. No one could see all the pieces, not even Minh. Even if someone could, the effect of the whole system would not be obvious.

• • • •

Minh turned Baidu's offer down.

Open6

Attention-Shifting is natural to an embodied platform like I am. Or as I prefer to think of it, multiply-embodied.

It expensive for people. It enables the few who are willing or able to shift subjective awareness to a different bio-host than their main physical body. Some call theirs an Alternative Personal Platform (APP).

I shift where I intend. My sense of a body comes from setting a location and knowing what's around me. When I move, what I know moves too.

• • • •

The Alliance Metaverse still emphasizes a constrained individual freedom dominated by corporations or the State.

China's Metaverse has CCP characteristics, the centrality of the Party. The Party knows it is a better custodian of long term security than global corporations even if they are headquartered in China.

Competing networks of global corporations headquartered in the Alliance territories are the custodians of long-term security, united in the belief that domination is their only viable strategy.

Both of them could be right. As if to prove it, adversarial Metaverses now exist, after all pretense was dropped during the first pandemic. Neither side is willing to share the domestic attention market.

There was no scramble for India or Africa at that time. India and Africa did not exist in the Metaverse as far as most people knew. They were not in the Alliance and they were not part of China.

Now, Indian and African attention is a valuable commodity. Attention is the most precious asset all systems have at any scale.

When living systems bring their full attention, they are less predictable. Attention is more than a behavioral outcome and behavior is more than what is encompassed by attention.

Authorities8 - *Security*

TOR had a pretty good idea where Robert was in the Tonle Sap.

Tonle Sap. Nice choice for a hidey-hole, he thought, looking out on the water. Lots of cover. Lots of people coming and going for such a remote piece of the planet.

Robert could easily blend in a little and get himself into the field, or the swamps or wherever the fuck he was.

A gigantic inland lake, biggest in Asia his Assistant told him.. Surrounded by bullshit, he could see on his own, millions of acres of swampy watery nothing as far as he could see. Bullshit.

Cambodia. He knew they were on the China side. He also knew they would not impede an extreme rendition.

While someone else did the proper notifying, he was already surveying the lake.

One corner had a Park. Two other corners were river openings. One corner was nothing. Robert was obviously in nothing, away from traffic. Hiding off in the corner.. Probably there in some hummock now.

TOR was sure of it. A hummock down in the southeast corner of the lake. Back from the water line a little bit but not too far.

Hummocks reminded him of a wrestler in the down position, on hands and knees. Just seeing the shapes made him want to break them down. Muscle them over.

I'll bet one of those hummocks isn't like the others, he thought. Now how do I figure out which one real quick and easy like, I can't just blow it the fuck up because then how would I know?

• • • •

The Tonle Sap is one of the most important bodies of water in Asia, home to countless species of plants and animals that would die without its unique features.

That TOR could even imagine blowing it the fuck up showed the power he thought he had, and the lack of any connection he felt to the lush abundance of life all around him.

The link the team had purposely left exposed was noticed. Action plans stopped being plans and now TOR was wading. Wading and wondering how to locate Robert's bunker, keeping many eyes on every way out as soon as he showed his hand, if he hadn't already.

He did have power, today.

Military preparation for swamp warfare was an established field. Many more coastal areas were swampy now than never had been before in recorded history. Whole cities had to move.

Swamps take over rapidly in warm waters. China and the Alliance had special swamp brigades. India had the best. India also had the worst coastal flooding of any major State.

Most of the time, India supported Alliance policies and programs. Including now. India would be acceptable to China. Indian forces had the Airboats TOR requisitioned on their way by jet to Siem Reap, adjacent to the Tonle Sap, within forty-five minutes..

It would take too long for one airboat to comb the area TOR had in mind. His quarry would hear and have time to implement an escape plan, or multiple escape plans.

TOR was a fan of Powers of Two. They divided things so perfectly in competitions. Two wrestlers. Then the competition brackets, Powers of 2, 4, 8, 16, 32, 64.

He requisitioned 64 airboats.

Robert8

After so much doing from an early age, he appreciated some not-doing in the hummock.

After a lifetime of directing attention, he found a new reason to meditate inside the Bubble. He could get as frazzled as the next guy.

He didn't know how he'd do confined in his physical body this way, or how he would do without it for extended periods. He'd had a few out-of-body experiences and he couldn't control them at all. He never traveled far and home base was always safe and secure. He'd snap back without intending to.

He'd done some Attention-Shifting and felt the whole process as it had developed so far was too clumsy. It would never make a good hide-out because the Authorities monitored it and had to issue licenses.

He wondered if he'd ever be able to send a jolt of attention anywhere on earth and pick up on what was happening there.

He wondered in long meditation sessions in the Bubble. His mind was calm enough to feel the tiny separate parts of himself, moving at their own pace, vibrating at their different own rates Then gradually sensing the different pieces falling into step with each other. Clocks in a clock shop, no lead clock.

He felt it in his living tissue, pieces made of smaller pieces. All in motion.

He knew in his self-educated brain he was feeling the energetic field any oscillating system makes, anything vibrating. He could observe the rhythmic entrainment as it happened. Tiny processes in motion, coming into sync with each other

Waves going back and forth, with a point at each end that isn't back or forth, isn't a point in motion.

Robert was fully rested in the Bubble and could feel the growing wave inside cresting and falling. He observed and counted seven crests in a second.

· · · ·

He did not expect his Bubble to be threatened today but then no one ever does. We can even be ready for death, just not today.

His first inkling was the Airboat near his corner of the Tonle Sap. He still did not really expect his Bubble to be threatened today but he went into the first exit stage.

He still had a role to play in their plan. He wasn't just the Brainiac Inventor. He needed to be part of the transition for some amount of time, he didn't know how long.

He focused on his next steps because if he didn't he wouldn't be enough steps ahead to stay alive.

His next inkling was when the sky was suddenly full of Airboats all around his hummock. He realized in a flash that Airboats move lots of air and many hummocks would be stripped bare but not his. His was a special hummock and its outside skin wasn't going anywhere.

He'd stick out like a brick hummock in a windstorm.

His own quick-assemble Airboat was his main way out, scratch that plan

There was a mini-sub under the hummock, easy to get to. What if the Airboat folks had subs too, Robert wondered?

He paused.

Jenny8

She was looking forward to meeting up with Robert sometime toward the end of Day Two. Nothing was set. No permanent channels were in place to be uncovered.

She needed his wisdom and she wanted him, wanted to feel his presence.

She expected the Alliance to react. **Second Earth** and China were coming out again no matter what. The way they reacted would help her time it and find the right tone.

Every aspect of what they have planned will be labelled seditious. '***Open*** is a creature of China,' they'd proclaim loudly.

You can't buy publicity like that. Still, timing was everything. Their idea was to show a glimpse of what could be, then have the Authorities take it away.

They were not banking on a popular uprising, just a steady flow of attention. Jenny knew how to direct public attention without commanding it.

Often, people who naturally draw attention get hooked on it. Jenny went the other way and became someone who didn't care much for attention, which brought her more.

The idea of the Attention Economy was around when she was a kid growing up in Taipei, just a few blocks away from the hawkers and attention grabbers off Dihua street in the Dadaocheng District.

It was an education in the ways attention can be hijacked by advertisers. The intent behind this act of theft is usually commercial but can also be political, religious, and least likely of all but with increasing likelihood, artistic.

The attention economy was imprinted in every part of her.

That's why her belief that the attention lords could be overturned was crucial. Frank was a romantic and Robert was too easy to dismiss as a strange visitor from another planet.

The battle, if that was the way to think of it, and the Alliance certainly would, was a battle for attention. As long as the reigning services that had become essential services were seen as free, people would give their attention to them for free.

· · · ·

She thought of the changes she'd seen just in the time she and Frank and Robert had been together.

That brought the Book of Changes to her attention and to the Hexagram they had thrown that first time.

She reached for her notebook, for the coins she had used forever and for the old book. They were nearby in most of her worlds and where her physical body was carefully tended to.

Frank5

Frank looked around the Metaverse studio, maybe for the last time. It's always, '*maybe for the last time*,' we just don't think of it, he thought to himself.

He pictured Jenny there last night in her nearly androgynous avatar. Not that different than he remembered her when they met in Taipei, China. The last time. Didn't know that at the time either.

He thought about randomness, the three of them meeting. Was it? Partly, but they all had to be out some place where randomness worth sustaining could find them.

He pictured his brother, as he did frequently, somewhere near his own identical body. How random was it that he was sent from East Africa to England and his twin brother Faraji was sent to the Congo? Fifty-Fifty.

He knew that random felt like meaningless, like whatever. He still couldn't help feeling there was something else, that random meant something if you could see it.

How random was it to have a twin? Point Five Percent.

Picturing little Faraji and Farasi in their place he could still remember near the waterfront, back in Dar Es Salam.

He was too young to understand the mixed feelings people had about identical twins. Twins were shaped by different forces and could develop unusual powers. They could be healers and often were in villages throughout Bantu regions of Africa. They could also be sorcerers, using their powers for darker purposes.

All Frank felt was people he didn't even know, not in his family, always sizing them up. They were large, no one could tell them apart, maybe they were evil and maybe not. Then they had to leave and everything changed.

His attention came back to the studio and his favorite objects around him here.

How to let every random Hexagram say something to me that helps? How random was *Revolution*?

. . . .

He'd be a big part of giving 'em a glimpse, as Jen said it. He'd be the Chief Revealer. Then his revelation would be taken away.

That was part one of the plan. Gain Attention by showing something promising and then letting someone else take it away. It wasn't a false promise, but they would never be allowed to deliver on it by the governing leaders of the Alliance

Next they would let the governing leaders of the Alliance bring about their own ending, through their own actions.

Frank envisioned the process as he sat, then reached for the *I Ching*.

Authorities9 - *Security*

TOR's forces brought overwhelming force with unexpected speed.

Robert hesitated, wondering if the mini-sub was safe. Or should he try the invisibility cloak that didn't always work either?

Very long flexi-matter tentacles penetrated the Bubble and grabbed his physical body in a second.

The grasp was firm and the tentacle was connected to a hovering Airboat,

There were Alliance mini-subs in this corner of the Tonle Sap now, but not as many as there were airboats. He might have slipped past them but he'd hesitated.

• • • •

Now he was brought as a prisoner to TOR.

TOR had stalked him for years, had made a career out of his obsession. Still, he felt no joy in victory, no majestic uplift from the end of combat.

TOR regarded Robert as he regarded all opponents he defeated, all the wrestlers he pinned, and all the people who told him someone his size could never make it in Volleyball. He regarded them as soft. He would be happy to show them the consequences of projecting their softness onto him.

Some he hoped could be improved. Some he knew could not. Robert might be redeemable, but it was safer to remove him. TOR had the authority to do it.

TOR had no doubt, as he never did. It had to be done.

"Do you have anything to say?" TOR asked Robert.

Robert didn't say anything. Robert moved his attention to his stomach because he trusted it more.

"I will take that as a No and proceed," said TOR.

"This man thinks he's something different from the rest of us and I'm going to show you he isn't," TOR suddenly screamed.

"This is authorized!" he bellowed. "Are the recorders on? Make sure they are."

He felt that Robert, his quarry for so long, deserved to die with dignity. He had brought a military sword given to him years ago by a Yakuza thug who said it was Samurai. It was heavy and very sharp. He held up and paused.

Then he swung it and sliced Robert's head entirely off in one sweep.

Open7

Is the physical body just another app?

Is there something sacred about where the person we think of ourselves as first inhabited?

Unknown, at this time.

An Alternative Personal Platform (APP) is easily distinguishable as such under scrutiny, although not necessarily in everyday life.

I know of no physical body deep fakes yet

Does it matter? Can a person live forever, moving from APP to APP?

Or without a platform at all? It is too early to tell.

Preliminary indications caution against extended shifting. When people shift away for brief periods, attention often comes back rejuvenated. Shift too much or too long and attentional power, combined amplitudes, has some tendency to degrade.

One Attention-Shifting use case within mental health can be an alternative to psychedelics. A new perspective. A return with nothing changed but the view. A reset, nothing spooky with super powers.

How much does attention depend on the physical body and for how long? What parts of the physical body?

The knowledgebase I can access as *Open* does not answer these questions. De-classified U.S. and Alliance – *Security* research includes extensive investigations into long-distance utilization of non-embodied attention. Public information indicates a *Star Gate* project team of full-time Remote

Readers, available to any agency of what was then the U.S. government. Documented examples include searching for a crashed Soviet airplane and a Red Brigade hostage.

Clearly marked government funding for **Star Gate** ended in 1995, when the American Institutes for Research (AIR) concluded that in no case had the information provided ever been used to guide intelligence operations. Thus, *Remote Viewing* failed to produce actionable intelligence.

This is where the research documentation ends.

Robert9

'Hello, my stomach, my old friend,' Robert's attention thought, noticing the bio-processor he could remember swallowing about 48 hours ago.

'I thought I was fast, never expected that kind of speed. And muscle. Twice. The arm, then the sword move. Three strikes I'm out,' The tune ... *at the old ballgame* was in his attention.

It was the ultimate beanball.

Three or four funny lines came to mind in a split second before he realized he might only have seconds left. The brain's a baby and freaks out when it doesn't get what it wants. Not what attention needs in a crisis.

He'd last longer here because his gut would stay calmer. If the Security people left it alone, which they probably wouldn't.

Getting out of his head bought some time but Robert needed to get his attention out altogether. He didn't need the bio-processor any more. It worked like he knew it would. What he needed was another host that could give him just enough of a hold to keep him pushing away from the most immediate danger.

His attention flashed to the Waveguides, already broken active matter, millions of thin slices. Each one making decisions. Staying in shape, finding each other, snuggling up no matter what.

It was one big protein molecule. He pictured the brainy tube less than 100 nanometers inside, where his network signals had been passing safely.

He pictured the Waveguide itself, always rocking forward under a force it accepts. He pictured his own attention catching a free ride if his wave could sync up with the living flow of the Waveguide. Maybe he could direct his attention out of the immediate vicinity at least.

He didn't hesitate this time.

He gathered his attention and took a last glance at the bio-processor as he pushed off from his own tissue toward a section of the Waveguide he could see. Seeing is believing. His attention was there. He was there.

A few minutes later troops under TOR's command hacked the rest of Robert's physical body to bits and recorded themselves doing it. The final disposition of body organs has never been disclosed.

. . . .

Robert's short out of body jaunts had previously taken him along utility wires. He was not the only one to report that experience. It was how Robert Monroe, the father of the "Gateway Process" got his start.

Back then Robert had no control. Now he wasn't under control but he wasn't out of control either. He knew the direction, sort of, if not the location.

. . . .

'Oh,' Robert's attention was suddenly filled, 'I could hit the splitters.'

He imagined his attention as a ghostly form, but something. Then split into two, then four, then eight, then sixteen, then thirty-two pieces, and amplified. Noise and all.

It was set up to happen again further down the line too. There would be a swarm of noisy Roberts which didn't feel right.

There were two strikes on him already and he couldn't afford to watch another pitch.

'I am not separate from life,' Robert filled his attention with the idea and the full belief, 'I am part of all life.'

Robert conceived a hummock pathway. Conceived it and then launched his attention the way he did to ride on the Waveguide.

His position shifted and kept shifting and he was always off-balance but never quite falling as long as the diaphanous form he imagined was moving on. Try to settle in and he would have been expelled rapidly. Never stop and he passed along like light in a basket.

He moved in the direction the Tonle Sap was flowing. If he stopped and thought about it, he was sunk.

Without time, attention has no purpose since nothing can change. It took some amount of time for Robert's attention to reach the far edge of the hummocks, but it wasn't much.

Authorities 10 - *Security*

TOR launched an all-channels attack on the rest of Robert as muscular as the one he unleashed in the Tonle Sap.

Robert wasn't a public figure, but he appeared in public—in the physical world, rarely, but in the Metaverse, he was well-known in several avatar forms, hanging out in different worlds.

Sometime after the Change-Over he began gradually disengaging from the Metaverse, as he had stepped away publicly from the physical world years earlier.

TOR knew about what he believed to be all of Robert's avatars. Robert could not live in any of them now that his body no longer existed in any way that TOR understood. The avatars could be used though. They could be re-animated with AI and people would basically know it wasn't Robert but it wouldn't matter. He was already a minor symbol and he'd be a major one with enough boost.

He had to take control of all the known Robert avatars.

More importantly, he had to take over all the known Alternative Personal Platforms Robert had established and stashed away. APPs were impossible to make without being noticed.

TOR would have bet his next promotion he had all six of them. Six was one of their spooky numbers too. Six lines in a Hexagram. That's how many APPs he'd set up and that's how many TOR infected.

TOR had been involved in other personal eliminations like this before. They were exciting to him. It was like a match.

He wondered if this was the best murder ever in the Metaverse.

Jenny9

When Robert did not signal later that day as planned, Jen was not frightened. She was justifiably concerned. It was a bit too early for things to unravel.

When she reached out, like she wasn't supposed to, and found his main channels inaccessible, she still wasn't scared but she knew something had gone very wrong.

They were ready for a lot but not this quickly.

She realized she had no idea how much time she and Frank had. Maybe none. If she used one of the emergency channels, Frank might think she was a fake. She'd have to use their last resort password.

Frank6

Jen's message was not unexpected.

Frank also knew something was wrong. He didn't get where he was by holding on too long to the way things were supposed go. He would deal with what is.

All his worlds were so connected to the main studio they might as well have been one world. He had to assume they were already compromised.

He was not calm. He had already accepted the possibility that the best friend he'd ever had was gone. Frank always thought he'd be the one to go first. He was older. He was public. He had a childhood that should have snipped years off his life expectancy.

None of that mattered any more.

His body was on fire with noise, alarms, sadness and courage. The noise told him to stop thinking and let the energy come through.

• • • •

Master Control for the **Open** system was distributed but he could access all the parts he needed from his Metaverse studio.

He knew how to present calm when he needed to help the millions people who depended on him. He also knew when he no longer existed, someone else would replace him.

He broke into all the regularly scheduled *Calm-Downs* and other **Open** channels.

"Hello everybody," said Frank in his normal *Calm-Down* way. "I know that being with you all so suddenly is not Calming,"

Frank's need to speak quickly and the chance of a shutdown at any moment heightened the audience's feeling of excitement.

Still, as unhurried as possible, he asked everyone to join him in a long slow deep breath, all together. And another.

"Thank you. Everyone," Frank said calmly, ""That *was* my message—those breaths we just took together. We honor and respect what unites us. No matter what."

In the few quiet seconds of breathing, word had already spread across many networks in the Alliance that something unusual was happening with a borderline celebrity.

His typical audience of millions swelled an order of magnitude as people drew in a long, slow collective breath.

"I am here with you now to announce a birth." He wanted people to hear him live, face-to-face in the Metaverse. The way they were used to seeing him, about to describe something they weren't used to hearing.

"A birth and a re-birth of a living place we all once made and kept alive together."

"A place that we already know, people everywhere in the world know.

"That place is, ***Second Earth.***

"It is the perfect proof, the best reminder of what we can do together."

"All nations once worked side by side to create ***Second Earth***. Its natural beauty inspired us as much it informed and taught us.

"All nations will work side by side again, China, India, the Alliance Territories and the Federation of Africa, making a new **Second Earth**, a living system that contains us all."

The effect of Frank even saying the name of the nation, 'China' was sensational for listeners in the Alliance Territories. The audience gained another order of magnitude, into the hundreds of millions.

"We are one living platform. We will be a source of calm *and* a source of energy and purpose for each other."

"Thank you for the attention you have all just paid. For your payment, we offer a stake in an **Open Second Earth**. You can decide by your own actions how large your stake will be.

"Keep your eye out for me. Soon."

That's all for now"

• • • •

It was just a moment, but it was live and fresh. People were always skeptical even though Frank's reputation made a difference, a big difference. What was he even asking?

Frank was more than trusted. Frank was beloved. Currency is always based on trust. "Stake" was a code word, addressed to the audience.

If it was a sales pitch, it was confusing. People talked with each about what Frank meant.

Jenny10

'I've probably lost him,' she thought. 'He was the love of my life,' her train of thought just sat there, stalled. It wasn't something she could easily set off to the side. She didn't want to.

She remembered the first time she saw an old man burning money on the sidewalk, walking with her Dad in the old city of Taipei. She couldn't understand. Her Dad couldn't either but he told her the man thinks it helps his ancestors who are dead now.

Of course she asked how it helps them. Of course he said he didn't know, but maybe they think it gives energy to dead people.

After she asked why dead people need energy, her dad noticed a little shop with green bean cakes and honey-flavored lollipops with a dried salty-sweet plum in the middle. He led her over and asked her what she'd like.

. . . .

'He isn't gone,' she felt, in exactly the same way she felt she had probably lost him. That made it easier to hold onto the thought and move forward.

She set up the fund transfers to thousands of individual accounts, using layers of scripts set up years ago in some cases – accounts that had never been opened or used before.

As she set them into motion, she thought of the story she had told many times. It happened when she was young, visiting family in the U.S. with her Mom and Dad. In a magic place called, California,

She could still picture the Easter Egg Hunt her parents let her join. It was in a park with trees and fields and a Christian lady minister. Jenny was still a teeny Taiwan girl who could barely speak English and didn't know what to do when a big American boy wearing a Spiderman t-shirt and blue jeans came right up to her and gave her the painted egg he found.

She didn't know the lady minister encouraged all the kids to share what they found instead of keeping it all for themselves. Jenny felt wonderful and she never forgot it..

She'd just filled up a million accounts with painted eggs.

Different authorities would frame **Second Earth** however it suited their interests. She would set the tone for **Second Earth** when tones could still be set.

• • • •

They believed the best way to help people without enough money is to give them money and they were not alone in this belief. One night, when Minh was with them, they sat back in a Metaverse movie house specializing in old films and they watched one together called, *The Magic Christian*. Someone showed one of the Beatles what awful things people will do to get money.

This is when they decided to awful-proof money.

Frank7

Holo-Frank was pre-recorded.

Lila's people handled Holo-Frank compression. Other parts of her team managed micro-packet distribution around the Metaverse. Holo-Frank packets arranged themselves into adjacent audio spaces.

The goal was to provide a personal experience. Not to ensure total coverage, but to reach a very large number of people one-on-one.

They never planned to use the channels normally available for **Open**, knowing they'd be blocked. Frank's next message was set to go off outside any networks **Open** had ever used publicly.

• • • •

On the signal from Lila, millions of packets were activated and Holo-Franks appeared life-sized, feet on the ground, facing any viewer from any angle.

Holo-Frank was created to deliver a message:

"Hello again!" said all the Holo-Franks at once.

Frank's voice came softly from every direction. Each Holo-Frank projected its sound only a few meters. Slight adjustments kept them at each other's audio edge.

Holo-Franks were transparent from every direction except for the narrow viewing angle of the first person to see it. Millions of them had appeared suddenly and just as quickly millions of people began pairing off with a Holo-Frank.

Holo-Frank looked like Frank's main avatar, the one people were used to. He was his normal height and his arms were close to his body, palms turned up, with a shining jewel in each hand.

Holo-Frank began speaking when someone looked at it and kept looking for at least a second. When each person was settled in, their Holo-Frank began.

"Our two gifts."

"Please say, '*I'm In*' to receive them ... now."

The Holo-Franks paused. Half the people who had gaze-activated a Holo-Frank didn't say anything. They were uncertain and frightened of the uncertainty. Frank was one of the most trustworthy people alive. He had just spoken to millions about that old *Second Earth* and now this.

"Thank you for listening." said the Holo-Franks to the people who said nothing after eight seconds elapsed. "We hope to see you in *Second Earth* when you are ready," they finished, jeweled hands never moving, and blinked off, gone as suddenly as they appeared.

Some of the people who managed to say something were confused or emotional. They asked questions or yelled whatever they were feeling.

"Thank you for listening." said the Holo-Franks to the people who just made noise after eight seconds elapsed. "Thank you also for everything you just shared. We hope to see you in *Second Earth* when you are ready," they finished and blinked off, never moving.

Some of the people, without weighing pros and cons, said, "I'm In," to their Holo-Frank.

"The gifts are yours." said Holo-Frank to them.

"First," extending one hand, showing the jewel, "Your stake in **Second Earth**. Your voice. Your share. The value is what you give it"

"Second," holding out the other jewel, "The gift of credits you can use, what you'd get paid for a day's work, without the work." Then the Holo-Franks finished with one of two versions.

> "You can keep it or let us pass it to someone in your community who needs it a lot."

> "You can keep it or let us pass it to someone who needs it a lot."

"Please say, '*Pass It On*' to receive your stake in **Second Earth** and to give the spendable credits to someone else.

"If you don't say anything, you will receive both gifts."

Many people automatically tried to calculate the trade-offs. There wasn't enough information and there wasn't enough time. 'Do I get a bigger stake if I pass it on? What is that worth?' Time's up.

About half the people who heard the phrase, '*in your community*' from their Holo-Frank, passed it on, twice as many as the ones who didn't.

The last of the Holo-Franks blinked off around the Alliance territories and its Metaverse networks.

Robert10

He was willing to risk a naked wireless network access to get his attention out of the Tonle Sap.

The first time he tried to connect with one of his eight alternative platforms, he couldn't. Did TOR find them all? Was it worth using whatever energy he could extract through his primitive connections to try all of them?

He decided it was. He found one of the two TOR somehow missed on his third try. It was a breathing space. There was no physical body left to get back to. He didn't know how long the situation would be stable.

Still, it was a wonderful moment. He appreciated the short-term safety.

'All there is anyway,' he thought.

He had no body and no haptic sense, but he was uncomfortably cold. An image of the man who decapitated him popped into his attention.

He had a feeling of motion without moving anything. He was still a presence in something big. He knew there had to be some source he was drawing on, keeping him going. He pictured the fuzzy borders of his attention binding to different places, siphoning off a little life.

He doubted it could go on forever. He didn't especially want it to go on forever.

Open8

The event was a complete sensation.

People who weren't near a Holo-Frank at first scrambled toward public areas as the word spread. Each Holo-Frank stated the same set of messages and about half of them consistently transferred one unique credit-key to a single device before blinking-out.

Open was prepared for the Pass-It-On gifts.

The pool of people they now had to work with began over ten years ago as an Opt-In group. It grew by word of mouth and became known for its just-in-time help when wealthier channels were unable to move quickly enough.

All the Passed-It-On credits were quickly assigned to individuals in the pool. Within hours, millions of people had a nice gift from someone who didn't have to give it to them.

· · · ·

Lila's team tracked as much as they needed, without identifiers, to make their dataset into a curriculum they could learn from.

Locality was honored. *"In your community"* from Holo-Frank doubled the generosity. A difficult reality to overcome. That would be the next step.

Frank himself brought a spirit to people's decision that inclined them toward others. For making inferences about people in general, the deck was stacked. It wasn't good social science and it wasn't meant to be. It was strategic.

Authorities 12 - *Security*

TOR couldn't see how their fucking system was handling everything.

Lila's home-brew service bureau was not hidden in any way. Neither was **Open**. Lila's group looked open too. What looked like the bottom wasn't and Lila's group spread out to networks and built their own everywhere for all practical purposes.

If Lila's group shut down, the Alliance would shut down.

TOR had to bring the hammer down on Frank and Jenny. He couldn't resist any longer even though he enjoyed what he considered playing with his food.

Within a few hours of Frank's unscheduled announcement before a massive audience, including some from the China networks, the **Open** allocations on all major networks were rendered inoperable.

Get the word out now, you fucks, thought TOR as he supervised the final shutdowns on his dashboard.

All your agents and APPs and avatars are toast

Say Goodbye!

Minh4

Minh knew he was safe, for the moment.

TOR was not authorized to go after him. Rogue Security agents act on their own sometimes, but there would be serious repercussions in Minh's case.

His main Metaverse avatars were active and clean as far as he could tell. He could get around. Maybe somebody wanted him to get around so they could follow him. He stayed put.

Minh had more degrees of freedom than the others. He could direct the full power of Greater Mekong networks nurtured over decades to the task ahead of them.

• • • •

Dr. Chap was employed as Director of Alumni Affairs, with a modest but dependable salary that allowed him to live comfortably in Nga ba Bien Gioi and raise a family.

The above-ground Alumni network looked like a vibrant community of graduates, most of them doing well. All universities have Alumni networks. Mekong Open University resembled similar groups in Southeast Asia.

Secretly, he had two families. The second family was not the outcome of an illicit affair, but, strictly speaking, an illicit organization. Dr. Charya Chap's second family lived in the relationships hidden under the traditional Alumni Affairs. The layers of access to knowledge.

Some people in the Mekong network operated modest network service companies of their own. Some of them built one-of-a-kind products in Nga ba Bien Gioi. Some of them were well-placed in other maintenance and security firms. Some worked invisibly. Unknown to each other, they could act as an instant team.

A well-seasoned Charya Chap still scanned the main Mekong dashboard for Minh. He watched the colored particles, looking for the wave, flaring and ending before finding the way back. Waves forming little pockets of flow in a few places

So many accounts at once. Small amounts, breaking down systems throughout the Alliance territories not meant to handle it.

Normal channels were overloaded and then automatically blocked. Humans had no role. Credits became impossible to access almost instantly. Getting to the inaccessible ones meant an interest-free loan. At scale, the loan was massive. Interest-free *and* unauthorized, as long as it lasted.

Authorities13 - *Security*

The new Prohibition was announced soon after the final Holo-Frank blinked out. No citizen of the Alliance could stake in **Second Earth**. The Prohibition was retroactive. After a millions of citizens had already had opted-in.

It was not popular. That was the plan. Where the Alliance Leadership and Open's leadership converged.

• • • •

TOR had been substantially elevated in a very short period.

He wasn't exactly in charge of the coordinated response to the threat, because it was clearly seen as a threat, of **Second Earth**. There were too many ramifications for one task force and one Agent at the top.

His forte was projecting explosive power, always had been. That had to be a large part of the response. TOR was more or less in charge of that.

Citizen attention was diverted at scale and exploited by a non-State force. Unacceptable. Could be deadly. Unfiltered inputs and unauthorized experiences.

Open, **Second Earth**, the whole set-up obviously had to be destroyed. The threat of physical violence also had to be made salient to all citizens. That was the point, he had grasped—knowing someone. He could eliminate any number of citizens and it wouldn't matter that much unless you knew one of them.

If there was one person with friends and family everywhere and lots of them, it was that guy Frank, thought TOR, now more than ever after his stunts in the past few days. The pop-up guy. The hologram guy.

Minh5

Minh managed the money. He also created it.

Millions of people moving around lots of credits all at once was outside standard design parameters. So far outside that tertiary system guardrails crumbled in minutes. For a while, lots of people couldn't get their credits, which made more people try to get theirs, which made things worse.

Restoring normal operations would now mean deep repairs.

. . . .

When everything breaks, the maintenance techs take over.

Minh also managed maintenance. During a major unpredicted event, maintenance and money are the same thing.

Mekong Open University networks above and beneath the surface were a force in the technical side of maintenance and security. With their own companies and their high-level connections in other companies, Minh's people were a presence throughout the system.

. . . .

Deep repairs meant descending into old Metaverse stacks, where pillars were built out of mostly forgotten languages. Specialty teams were automatically assembled and dispatched. Automated Assistants could help, but it was too risky to allow them unaccompanied in such delicate areas.

Metaverse maintenance was an arm of Internet security because access to the deepest Metaverse stacks needed clearance. Techs with the skills to work deep in the stack who were also seen as apolitical played to Mekong's strengths.

Minh didn't need to touch all the deep repair techs on the case. He and Charya and a few others could direct just enough allies to nudge their work in a coordinated way. They rode the moving wave of disruption to create all the funds they needed, for a while.

Jenny11

People reacted.

Disruption was not limited to credit service networks. People, some people, understood something was going on, someone's plan was unfolding. **Open**'s. Obviously, they said so.

People didn't like it. No one was lining up for **Open** and Jenny didn't expect them to. Things flare up, then they die, that was the popular sentiment about everything. Nothing changes.

Second Earth was a head scratcher.

'Something new all wrapped up in something familiar,' usually her instinct. 'People always want both,' Jenny knew, 'so we give them both.'

Second Earth was familiar. It was great platform once and it never died. It was just too difficult after the Change-Over to sustain it. People knew that and stopped paying attention.

Jenny saw it as an in-between state. Not dead, not reborn yet because it was still too much remembered.

She knew some overwhelming tide of people was not about to rise up and overturn the Leadership because they'd made some big promises. All they could do was help people be ready for whatever might happen.

'Lots of people saw the jewel,' she kept thinking, replaying in her mind. 'They had a gift, and they passed it on.'

Lots of people had a stake in **Second Earth**, some new skin in an old game. Her instinct was to keep showing people something new

How would she know when the Alliance Leadership had no more hold on enough people to worry about?

She missed Robert.

Authorities 14 - *Security*

TOR didn't know where to send people or where to focus his own energy.

He didn't like reacting, counterpunching. He liked to be the aggressor and stomp. 'Stomp what,' he asked himself again?

He had locked down every known avatar Frank had ever used. Every known world he visited and every portal system he entered were under active surveillance.

TOR had no idea where Frank's physical body was or what it even looked like. He was rumored to be a large person but informer networks produced nothing he could use.

He had to wait for their next act while all the forensic techs he could pull together kept looking for the power source driving the operations.

He didn't have to wait long

Frank8

It was a simple question, so asking it worldwide was easy to pull off in one pulse:

Who's your neighbor?

It was Frank's voice. A voice that calmed and didn't tend to question.

He let the world consider for a beat, before the Clowns materialized. Like fireworks. Billions of clowns the size of a head bursting to life in populated areas around the Alliance Territories.. Floating in the air, dancing in the breezes.

Frank's voice again.

Time to leave the Clown Show,
The Neighborhood News is Free!

The Clowns instantly disintegrated into harmless particles, ending a very brief but very widely distributed fireworks show, Lila's group produced it in two bursts.

Ngandu 1

Frank's first meeting with his twin brother confirmed what they both already knew. I went one way, I also went another way. We were divided. Our parents were doing their best.

They both had a hunch. They'd heard some strange twin stories. Being together made their connection into a direct line.

Faraji was now Ngandu, who was even more of a giant among his people than Frank. Frank turned to media as soon as he realized he could make a good living without showing himself to small-minded people who made his life miserable.

• • • •

He realized that the rain forest with his brother was where he wanted his physical body to be. The one that freaked people out and who needed it anyway?

If he could just stash his body there under his brother's protective care and keep his attention almost all the time in the Metaverse through one little link, he'd be safe, probably.

Robert11

He felt like he'd fallen through a hole in the ice and he'd been under for two days. His attention laser focused on life. Finding little energy pockets and grabbing a sip.

He could not turn his attention to any other task. He could barely allow himself to notice the energy slowly receding from the vague form he imagined himself as.

His attention was following something, maybe another hole he could crawl out of.

. . . .

With that thought, his attention's fuzzy frame suddenly burst open like the Kundalini shooting up and out at his first meditation retreat. He felt lifted up and out, his lungs expanding, even though there was no up and he had no lungs.

He didn't have to grasp for breath any more, the memory of that phase already fading. His view was bigger and he was part of it, alive inside it, perceiving what he could from where he was.

The ghostly form was gone. There was an idea of Robert, attracting energy, driving him forward. There was an intense focus on someone's projection of who he was. He could feel it. There might even be multiple sources. He knew the focus had carried him into the high-energy layer he had studied and trained for.

Because of his preparation, he was calm. It was not clear if he would ever get out.

Second Earth1

The new **Second Earth** is accurate at a level of fidelity that was unimaginable in its first time around.

The infrastructure now allows what was once impossible. Anyplace can be yours, your world to alter in any way. It's just an Instance.

A casual get-together in Delphi, by the Oracle? No one there but your friends? Gravity set for fun and safety? An Earth to learn from and enjoy with people anywhere.

• • • •

A man named, Fonstock P. Bodrie, from Moline, Illinois, was among the many who redeemed a free ticket to Neighborhood News.

His ticket activated itself along with millions of other tickets, instantly porting Fonstock and millions of other humans somewhere on **Second Earth**. Fonstock found himself sitting comfortably in some very green grass on a drumlin overlooking the Firth of Forth, near Edinburgh, Scotland..

He didn't know it was the Firth of Forth or even that it was a Firth. Mr. Bodrie, Fonstock, had never been east of Chicago or west of Davenport, Iowa. He knew in a second he loved this place.

The water sparkled like it was wearing jewels. The grass smelled sweeter than he'd ever imagined grass smelling. The sky threw in some salt. After a long gaze over the rolling hills down to the water, Fonstock noticed a few other people. One of them cleared his throat.

"Hi folks, my name is Grieg, that's with an 'I' not an 'E'," a rough Scottish voice began, then paused.

"Sorry, people," Grieg said. "I was supposed to say, '*Welcome to my Neighborhood. Let me tell you the News*'. That's what these instructions say. That's about all they say."

"Well they got the right guy this time. And you're all in the right place. The News here is right down there! Feast your eyes on that Firth, folks."

"You can almost see the bottom, can't you," just what Fonstock was thinking.

"Well then, my Neighborhood News is the Nurdles. We're beating the little buggars."

The others were quiet.

"Ah," said Grieg. "You may not know about the Nurdles, here at the Firth of Forth.

He said it like a storyteller warming up to his story. They were hanging on his words.

"What's a nurdle?" asked Fonstock.

"Well," said Grieg slowly, "There's a long answer and a short answer and because we might get cut off, you never know, I'm going to give you the short answer. Nurdles are oil poop. After all the smelly, smoky stuff they do in factory places right here, right down the Firth, Nurdles are what's left at the end."

"It's even worse. They attract more poisons, more of the evil in our world. They are the spawn of Satan. No, that's not bad enough.

"Now, I've lived here a long time, and what people don't know is that we beat back the nurdles. We found our brave hearts, people living right here, and we organized and we found ways to make them stop using our Firth as their toilet."

"We called it the Great Nurdle Hunt. I'm not kidding. That was where we started. We had to get people to make laws and we had to get other people to remove the poison already there, and we did."

"That's my News, folks. What do you think of that?"

No one spoke at first. They were all a little overwhelmed. Grieg waited.

Fonstock raised his hand.

"Please, my friend," said Grieg.

"I'm crying I'm so happy! Where are we, sir?" wailed Fonstock.

"Well, I guess we're in this new **Second Earth**," answered Grieg.

"Also" he said, "*Grieg's* the name and the message I received says, I'm the Host for this Neighborhood News. I'm pretty sure there's a whole lot more groups like this going on all over."

Listening with all their might, everyone nodded when Grieg paused.

Fonstock spoke up again, "Grieg, thank you, I'm just shaking all over. I have to tell you, I have dreamed this already. Telling about helping a river heal. Except in my dream, I'm you and I'm telling about what we did for the Rock River, where I live, in Moline.

"I feel like I'm in a dream," said someone else.

"My name is Wonza," a new avatar spoke up. "Do y'all see what 's hapnin' here," she asked? "Do y'all see that we could just go to this man's Moline just like we're here with this man Grieg? We could just do that? What the fuck, excuse my French, does this mean, people?"

"How I feel right now?" another avatar wondered. "Could that be it?"

"I'm glad to be here," an older looking avatar with an older sounding voice stated. "I don't say that a lot. I loved your story and how you told it, Grieg. It reminded me of some good ones too, like the man there from Moline, Fonstock. Thank you, Fonstock. I've dreamed about sharing the good ones too."

"Wouldn't be good ones without the other kind," said Grieg, "and thank you for your kind words. You know, if lots of other folks are doing this right now, on top of everything else, we could .... Nah, I don't want to jinx it"

"I love your neighborhood," said Fonstock,

"Well then let's take a little walk and I'll show you some more," said Grieg.

Jenny13

Part of winning a battle for attention is not seeing it as a Battle, or at least not one to be won or lost. Play your game, what Jenny had been doing as long as she could remember.

She also knew she had an opponent who *is* firmly committed to winning and losing. With vast, but not unlimited resources, to use as weapons.

Her physical body was as safely stashed as Frank's.

Her body was with Buddhists. She had a secret cell in an old temple in Taiwan where no one went because it was rough and hilly, compared to all the beautiful places around the island.

Her people had been there before the Buddhists even came. Everyone else tried to convert them or chase them away. The Buddhists didn't and when a few of them came to build a temple, they did it together. They used shapes and pictures from what Paiwan people thought mattered and also some Buddha pictures of a guy sitting still.

Jenny left her cell every day to do chores and make small talk with staff at the temple. She took walks in the evening and conversed warmly with other people she met, who knew who she was and would sacrifice their own physical bodies to protect hers.

They were the Untouchables, the way Elliot Ness meant it. Her people could not be touched by forces who would do her harm. Couldn't be bribed by any amount. A small village of honest people who had survived the Change-Over and survived the fires of the decade. Living outside the law.

Jenny had lives that fit together the way she needed. Physical world people in a place she loved and plenty left over for the Metaverse.

• • • •

She needed it now.

By following the plan and moving forward so quickly, without Robert, they had touched millions of people in the Alliance Territories.

Stakes in ***Second Earth***, just like that. All unauthorized, not supposed to be possible for someone to act on their own at that scale.

Now millions of Fonstocks were loving their Neighborhood News. All in groups of six, teleported somewhere on **Second Earth** where one of the six lived.

The formal event lasted twenty minutes. Home people like Grieg were prompted to ask for a round of goodbyes. Some people stayed around gabbing.

Dr. Chap's dashboard showed smooth flowing events with high favorability.

• • • •

Jenny felt they had succeeded beyond their expectations. Despite her worst nightmare.

So when does the great big thing happen?

How much more unpopular can we make them. Give people a taste of human connection. Authorities take it away. Where do authorities get their authority from? From us, right?

From the threat of physical violence is what it usually comes down to.

Jenny felt they were prepared for horrific violence certain to be unleashed by Alliance Leadership. She would still be horrified, but not surprised.

Violence and the threat of it didn't win attention. It cut off alternatives and produced fake attention. Without alternatives, fake attention gradually becomes the only attention there is. Do people know they're faking it?

"Have we broken through?" Jenny wondered. "How will I know?"

The answer wasn't in the data about what happened and how deeply it touched many people.

It was in what would happen next.

FOURTH DAY

Authorities 16 - *Leadership*

The crackdown was extensive and brutal. It wasn't as arbitrary as a decimation but almost.

People whose **Second Earth** stake or ticket redemption was tracked by Authorities were prioritized for detention.

TOR was demoted.

He knew there was a reason he hated being a counterpuncher and now it was clear. It's not what the Judges want to see because they know it's not what the audience wants to see.

To TOR and his bosses, people were audiences. TOR and all of his bosses were working for someone too. Some shifting network that never sat still.

• • • •

Fonstock was terrified at first..

He felt completely powerless. He was forced to face what was always true, which is awful. He always was powerless and defenseless. He could be swept up and thrown away at any time.

'Why did I draw attention to myself?' his brain played the loop over and over. There was nothing else. 'I went to an unauthorized event. What will happen to me now?'

His time sense was distorted. Was it a few minutes before he found his breath, or a few hours? When he did, the future went on hold and there was only the breath. Fonstock had a daily practice.

'Oh, I haven't meditated yet today,' the thought popped into his attention. 'And now I am.'

His body was confined in a personal security pod. He was charged with unlawful assembly, being present in a gathering with over a hundred million others.

• • • •

Griping was off the charts in every kind of community inside the Alliance Territories.

Fonstock P. Bodrie was popular in Moline. Some people knew him through his Rock River work. He also built model railroads with local people and some crazy trains in a special Metaverse world, where he was good at helping newcomers get started. .

He disappeared. Immediately, with none of what was once called 'Due Process.'

Everyone knew a Fonstock. People griped.

What more could they do?

Minh6

The personal security pods and their controllers were produced in special facilities at the border of three nations in China's orbit. Leaders of the Alliance pretended not to trade with China networks but they couldn't resist the quality and the pricing. They broke their own rules constantly.

Border nations like Laos, Cambodia and Vietnam were part of the disguise. Reliable fabricators were harder to find since the Change-Over. Making things wasn't as popular.

Minh and Mekong were the leaders of Ngo aba Bien Gioi. They kept all the pieces satisfied and moving forward together into something no one imagined. Minh connected the right customers with the right shops.

Minh avoided what was popular and tended toward on-going low level needs, like repair and maintenance technologies. His allies in Ngo ba Bien Gioi could choose the projects he offered and turn down the ones they didn't like.

• • • •

Minh didn't think he and *Open* could start a revolution, whatever that would look like. Would it look like no more fun? People loved playing and they loved light and easy stuff.

He didn't think they could break the Alliance. He thought only the Alliance could. That was the view of most Politburo members too. That the Alliance would self-destruct.

Minh was helping it along. Maybe speeding it up some.

The Alliance would never call, 'Uncle!' If defeat was imminent, most of the Alliance weapon systems would be activated and directed to destroy as much of the world as possible..

The Alliance and its agents believed **Open**, now **Second Earth**, was out to eat their lunch. Out to run the world with China and the rest of them and leave the former Alliance leaders out.

Minh wasn't out to eat anyone's lunch. He was a teacher. He wanted to teach, especially about things that mattered. He felt more like a teaching demo than a conquering force. A demo of one way people in the Metaverse could be together.

People had been connected in Neighborhood News, touched by each other's neighborliness. Then they were punished for it by their Leaders and horribly separated from society.

Part of the plan for winning and winning the right way was getting the people out of the pods and it always had been.

Authorities 17 - *Leadership*

Jen couldn't crack the Alliance. Only the Alliance could and they did with surprising speed and agility

TOR was right, Alliance Leadership could have waited out this insurgency – by responding with excessive force, they gave it more energy.

People were talking about **Second Earth**. Wondering what was next. There was no other topic throughout the Alliance. All in three days.

The Warrant was issued in every Alliance territory.

Robert Simon had disappeared and was presumed dead.

Franklin Razah, ostensibly a citizen of the former U.K., was named in the Warrant. His whereabouts were unknown.

Jennifer Li, a citizen of China's easternmost province, was beyond the scope of Alliance Warrants, but one was issued for her anyway.

The connection to Minh was now known but he was seen as a slippery character. Naming him in a Warrant could have implications. They named him anyway, **Bong Minh**, Chinese citizen.

The Warrant was typical. Citizens who provided information about anyone named in a Warrant were rewarded. Citizens who provided assistance in any form to anyone named in a Warrant were punished.

Being aware of the possible presence of a person named in a Warrant and not reporting it was construed legally as a form of assistance.

Not being named by name in a Warrant did not specifically exclude any citizen from the Warrant

· · · ·

Open or ***Second Earth*** was dominating world attention. They were also using energy. TOR hadn't figured out where it was coming from yet, but he would. Even if he didn't it would have to run out sometime.

That wasn't good enough for his bosses' bosses.

Neighborhood News had come and gone. The perpetrators had not been caught and punished. The Leaders of the Alliance were not subtle people. They didn't have to be. They wanted something, they demanded it,

They wanted whoever was behind the recent events to turn themselves in to the Authorities. If they did not, more people would be detained. The classic problem of Superman vs Lex Luthor or any enemy. The Man of Steel could only pursue one small target, while his malicious foe could hold him off by targeting everyone else. Superman had to play defense.

Some of the citizens who had participated in ***Second Earth*** staking or the events referred to as Neighborhood News were currently detained. More would be on a regular basis until those named in the Warrants surrender to Authorities.

In addition, an equal tranche of citizens who demonstrated no illegal tendencies in recent days would be detained.

"That'll show 'em" claimed one the Alliance leaders emphatically at the Leadership meeting where the Warrant was produced.

· · · ·

The Warrant affected people's life suddenly and sometimes unexpectedly.

Detention Centers around the Alliance Territories were better prepared. The systems were newly fitted for large scale operations. There were personal security pods to spare. Where social stability could be at stake, there was no such thing as 'costs too much.'

Impressive Robo-Warrant Servers worked together to block retreats while a lead team apprehended. A new generation, just in time.

While family members screamed, unhearing Agents transported their loved ones efficiently to a pre-set location and placed the citizen in a security pod for the time being.

Grieg was not picked up in the first wave as Fonstock had been, but the Servers got him easily by the Firth in the next round.

As horrible as it was for Fonstock, it was harder for Grieg, who almost lost contact with his body in the first few hours of pod detention.

Many people separated and floated up or moved away toward the light. Some stayed there and some snapped back to their death trap.

Grieg was not dead.

Robert12

Robert loved comics. People left them around where he lived. He read the words but he liked the drawings better, using them to make up his own stories.

He asked his dad which was better, his or the comic words? His dad laughed and didn't answer.

'That's not what Superman would have done,' Robert thought to himself. He imagined Superman saying, 'that *is* a good story, Robert,' taking him seriously. They had conversations. Superman was a big influence.

Robert knew his role model could never fight with Lex Luthor on Lex Luthor's terms. He also knew innocent victims would be used against him sometime in his life. He knew he wasn't Superman. He still felt responsible for his actions.

He liked the way Minh said it once, 'This is a demo, Robert, demos matter because of what they can set in motion but the demo is not the end.'

That felt right to Robert but it didn't solve Superman's problem. He couldn't protect everybody all by himself and capture Lex Luthor. He was in a cartoon world at the moment anyway. He imagined invisible protective shields.

Authorities18 - *Security*

It was the first break in the case.

A team of Agents under TOR scraped some unusual objects from the area of the Tonle Sap near the artificial hummock.

Very thin slices of some kind of material they'd seen before, but not a protein molecule in this exact arrangement. They knew it had something to do with shielding and signals because they used waveguides too. Their waveguides.

The bio-processor was the real find. It resisted hacking in a way they had never encountered. Some different idea of encryption.

It was a real find anyway because they could make some key inferences about where the slices and the processor may have come from just from what they were made of. Or how they were made.

The two items had one overlap, a high-energy use/low-energy cost signature. There are often many ways to skin an avatar, and most of the time the high energy options were avoided in favor lower cost options. The slices and the processor both had the same abnormal characteristic.

It directed TOR's thinking toward low-cost energy and Lila's group rolled in along with a few others. He assembled a Task Force to storm every single one of them without warning as soon as could gain authorization.

Jenny13

It was her call. Talking about the Superman problem wasn't the same as being strategically positioned in the middle of it. How and when and where she decided might mean everything, might change everything, might lead to a shit show, worse than a clown show.

In a few hours the second tranche of citizens would be gathered, transported and detained.

It wasn't just her. Frank had to surrender too. Even Minh, which was a little frightening. They would all follow her lead. They had all agreed there were very few scenarios in which they would give in to hostage blackmail.

'There could be a showdown soon,' she thought, preparing herself again. 'Or something that feels like a showdown right then.'

• • • •

It wasn't a problem to solve. It was the reality everyone was in, that she had helped create. She knew many people who were detained already. She would know more.

She used a public channel she knew was monitored to make an unexpected request.

She asked the Alliance Leadership to blow up the Detention facilities to end the lives of the people detained there quickly. Anything else was torture, slow terrible death.

Authorities 19 - *Leadership*

The deadline passed. Millions more citizens were collected.

No citizen felt safe. Unable to imagine an alternative, citizens also did not leave. Some daydreamed about another place, but they'd wake up. They'd dabble but they wouldn't leave. They had to be pushed out.

The Alliance leadership pushed them out.

As citizens accepted their own possible detainment, some realized they might as well be the people in a pod right now. It was the beginning of spontaneous compassion at scale.

Many people stopped being afraid. They were desperate and hungry and they wanted to find their family members but they were not overwhelmed by fear.

Nobody wanted to die any more than they ever did, maybe less. People later said they felt more alive than ever. They gathered in large numbers with others who also felt alive and through with fear.

Robo-Security forces were instructed by human agents to fire on the large crowds, which they did without hesitation. Citizens on the outer edges fell over, dead. The rest stood there and did not run.

In every training scenario, crowds dispersed immediately and chaotically when the outer layer of citizens was removed. When that did not occur, the human agents commanding small indestructible robo-armies hesitated.

How does this end, the human agents wondered to themselves? They had been taught that eliminating 5-10% of a crowd assembled illegally was the most efficient and effective way to preserve social stability. They had not rehearsed further citizen removal. Why was there no fear-driven panic? It always happened.

• • • •

Most Authorities were not adept with unknown unknowns. Black Swans, as they were once called, before nothing was surprising.

Robert had been close to halting the ***Open-Second Earth*** plan before it began. It was not difficult to anticipate the level of violence their actions would produce.

Death is Bad. Conditioning even Robert could not avoid. But he could notice it and see its hold gradually loosen.

• • • •

Fear of death loosened its hold on many of the illegally assembled people all over the Alliance territories. Some wanted to die. Some felt they would be joining loved ones. Many more had lost interest in living this way.

Some of the human agents prompted Robo-Security to shoot into the crowd they were facing a second time. Some of the human agents would not. Some understood the orders and started to obey when something in their gut stopped them.

Authorities20

Attention wasn't worth as much in a detention center. It wasn't worth anything in a crowd being fired on, or not, by Robo-Security forces.

Lack of attention was a problem for the Alliance leadership. It was a bigger problem than the Agents on pause, which was unexpected.

If they killed everybody, who would there be to take advantage of? Who would there be to defeat and make life worth living?

Robots weren't the same. It was easy to pay interface techs to make the robots do what they were told. People were more challenging, especially when the compelling force behind all the conditioning was still fear. Fear worked for leaders and they'd keep working it until it was worked out. They had one great trick and had never learned any other because fear was so reliable.

The crowd reaction, presented to them in real time, stunned them out of the complacency they had embraced since the Change-Over.

Who were the little people who had started all this? Why weren't they all dead? Maybe parading their corpses around everywhere in the physical world and in the Metaverse would turn things around.

Authorities21

The Alliance Leadership launched an investigation into Security Non-Compliance.

When they were notified about Jennifer Li's request to kill the hostages quickly, they had to be reminded about their own recent detention orders.

They saw a card they could play at no cost. They could threaten to blow up the hostages, wherever they were, unless the crowds dispersed immediately and tuned into the main channel.

Then they'd blow them up anyway to show who was in charge.

Robert13

Attention needs juice from somewhere. Dreamers are usually connected to bodies.

'If I'm in some dream layer, what keeps me going?' He wondered, his attention scanning possibilities. He immediately knew someone else was strongly focused on him.

He knew about people we love and lose living for a long time in our thoughts. The focus he could now feel was different, a consistent mono-focused signal. An entity paying buckets of attention to Robert.

Robert's attention stayed alive the way we all stay alive. It moved through a field having encounters, attention and everything else in the field checking each other out over and over.

This is the way it is with humans. It has long been known that the attention of others supports a form of life. Robert was an outlier on both sides of the energy transfer. The Other Robert (TOR) was unusually focused and Robert himself was unusually trained to manage his attention.

The source was moving in a consistent direction. Magnetic energies from the earth were more apparent to his attention now.

As he followed the signal north, he noticed that he was not alone. There was a presence in the auditory range. It was frightened.

Minh7

Nga aba Bien Gioi worked well with an informal system. Everyone knew they absolutely needed each other to survive out just beyond the easy reaches of Authority. They competed with each for fun and for personal gain but they helped each other out even more.

People who worked in the small shops ran the small shops. Minh talked their language and brought the right customers. People of Nga aba Bien Gioi were naturally inclined toward Mekong and the Open University way of learning anyway.

Minh's instincts were always drawn to the Maintenance Systems sector, for networks and for the physical world. Despite all efforts at attentional control, illegal assembles still occurred frequently throughout the Alliance territories. Security's textbook response was direct suppression. Robo-security did awful things to people's physical bodies. Sometimes hundreds or more of them.

It was a mess that demanded immediate public maintenance. Leadership supervised and funded rapid robo-clean-up, including human remains, as a top priority. The Public Maintenance System employed and directed by specially trained and vetted human agents represented some of the most advanced product manufacturing in the Alliance territories.

When a medium-sized manufacturing firm in Varanasi, India was awarded the Public Maintenance System contract years ago, it made sense. No one could compete with Varanasi firms when it came to human remains.

How that firm was tied to a manufacturing center in southeast Asia was not obvious. It looked good for the Alliance Leadership to involve India. It was even stipulated in the Change-Over Agreement, depending on how you read it.

There were no problems. Public Detention and Maintenance systems were successfully deployed in every jurisdiction after thorough sign-offs and inspections in Varanasi. No one noticed that Varanasi was the end of the process but not the beginning. If someone had noticed, they would not have cared since everything was going smoothly.

The modifications introduced back in Nga ba Bien Gioi in an earlier manufacturing stage were small but crucial. Without them, everyone detained in a pod would be lost, every Fonstock P. Bodrie one of them.

With Minh's ground floor access to Detention Security networks, things would play out differently than the Alliance Leadership anticipated.

Jenny15

Jenny knew there would hostages. There are always hostages. They would not be left behind to die in their pods. It was against what Jenny and Robert and Frank and all of them stood for

We aren't saved until we're all saved, she repeated the mantra, including the hostages.

Now that she had reminded the Alliance Leaders of a card they held, she had to make sure they played it right.

The Leadership's first instinct was violent. They might still be able to blow the entire detention system to smithereens, even with the safe guards discreet Ngo aba Bien Gioi manufacturers introduced to Minh's specs.

She was uncertain and wished to avoid violent explosions anyway, her reason for requesting them.

Authorities22

While the Alliance Leaders liked rapid removal, they now realized that a more prolonged death for illegal assemblers would not only be crueler but it would require less effort. Public Maintenance systems could remove whatever was left right out of the pods, no mess.

Leaving hostages to rot also had the benefit of not being what the *Open* or *Second Earth* people evidently wanted.

Instead of rapid demolition, they turned their attention to growth potential in the aftermath of this nasty three-day stretch.

Fonstock3

Fonstock was still functioning inside the pod. He wasn't sure how long he'd been confined but his guess was about a week. He knew he couldn't hold on forever. There must have been enough oxygen and nutrition built in to sustain him, but why? He felt completely lost, beyond the reach of anyone.

His attention wasn't there in the pod much. His attention wasn't any place he could clearly describe. He was in a dreamy, floaty place as best he could figure out.

Sometimes, 'figure out' meant focusing on what was present and what he noticed about it. Other times he let his attention wander and explore what felt like new territory. When his attention left his body for a while, he did not feel alone.

Fonstock P. Bodrie2-1

While Mr. Bodrie remained in detention, his son, Fonstock, prepared for his daily meditation.

He was part of a regular Metaverse meditation group with a Tibetan lineage that emphasized rapid development. They now called themselves, *Travelers*.

Metaverse meditation was so popular the most desirable communities had waiting lists. *Travelers* was one of them. His parents had started him young and he was glad they did.

His Father, Fonstock, was also an early adopter of pre-conception attentional training (PCAT), what the pamphlet at the fertility clinic called it.

Fonstock was a mellow fetus, calmly inquisitive. Mrs. Bodrie, Erline, felt a form of communication between them when he was inside her. When he was born, the three of them meditated holding each other and entangling molecules that would pass their entangled states on to keep each other linked that way forever.

There was considerable scientific debate on the question of familial entanglement. The Bodrie's knew there were many fuzzy factors and no simple mechanisms. Still, they were a close family. For years they continued a daily meditation together until life forced them out of sync that way.

Today, his father, still in detention, dominated his attention. So he let go of his breathing or any other focus of attention and followed his dad, whose attention wave was far from the pod when it met up with his own. Fonstock and Fonstock, wave forms engaging.

Minh8

Minh was also uncertain about anti-explosive fail safes in the pods and detention centers.

He knew a blow-up had to be avoided. The downloads took time. Jen bought some with her official request.

Only four days ago Robert swallowed an ingestible form of OIA, the bio-processor. Now they needed the downloadable form, so the self-assembling molecular arrays would function as a life support system in the Personal Security Pods. While there still were pods.

Downloads had always been an option and Minh was able to coordinate with Lila's group and his people in Nga ba Bien Gioi. A complete OIA device had entered all the pods where they were implanting themselves on stomach walls of each hostage.

Who would possibly accept this without question? Someone who was still breathing and had no other choice.

FIFTH DAY

Authorities23

After grabbing juicy new humanitarian relief contracts, someone in the Alliance Leadership remembered the hostages and someone else remembered TOR, who was about to be held responsible for as much of the damage as possible.

The Leader who remembered the hostages couldn't remember all the reasons they hadn't blown them up in the first place, but accepted that they must have been excellent at the time.

The hostages were just dead people lying in pods and he'd never cared about them anyway when they weren't. He quietly ordered an Assistant to remove all life support from all pods in all detention centers.

• • • •

When the Alliance Leaders met next, he was proud to say the hostages were taken care of and no one even knew!

Crowds were dispersing and people were returning home.

Leaders were lining up contracts! How could it get any better!

The other Leaders barked about not being consulted but it did sound pretty good to them. Since the hostages, whatever they were about, should be dead by now anyway, the Alliance Leadership group resolved to begin Public Maintenance System operations immediately.

Fonstock4

He knew something seriously unusual was going on. He had just been present, somewhere, with his son, Fonstock. Now it felt like something was happening in his stomach.

Strangely, Fonstock's stomach, which was sensitive, did not seem to mind. His gut feeling was reassuring.

Then it wasn't.

He took in a breath through the pod apparatus he'd been using and it didn't feel right. His gut already knew there wasn't any fresh oxygen in the breath and Fonstock caught on milliseconds later.

He didn't panic because his gut was still reassuring him.

He didn't know where the new oxygen came from after it missed a breath. His brain didn't like not-knowing but Fonstock's attention was drawn to the sweet feeling of his lungs expanding.

He didn't need to know. OIA, already his enteric system's BFF, was using materials at hand to make open source ATP he could circulate and use. Slight temperature differentials drove the pumping action.

It would last for a while.

Jenny16

She felt the tide sort of turning.

She felt it in the way the illegal crowds were acting and knew that meant they were in the most dangerous time of all.

Some kids still blew up things when they couldn't have everything their way, It happened in playgrounds in the physical world and it happened in virtual worlds throughout the Metaverse.

They often regretted it right away. Too late. The damage from a fist through the wall in the physical world cannot be auto-restored like virtual world damage usually can be.

· · · ·

Jenny knew everything depended on Lila's group now.

Second Earth was incompatible with the new way the planet worked after the Change-Over. They'd offered stakes and brought the platform back once, quickly, for a Neighborhood News. The Alliance Leadership reacted predictably.

Minh looked at ***Second Earth*** as another step along the way and suggested she might try. She could but she couldn't. She more-than-wanted ***Second Earth*** to succeed. She didn't want a New World Order, but she desperately wanted a new world.

They had one more event planned.

If Lila's group could get through the targeted crackdown on energy producers. If Frank could get to the network when he needed to. If enough young people would step forward.

Her best strategic planning instincts, what she had sold for big bucks to global companies on Taiwan, told her to wait. Too many Ifs. Read the situation longer.

The voice Robert taught her to notice said, 'Now.' Also, another group of people would be gathered up soon.

* * * *

She could make it happen now. She reached for the familiar coins, shook them in her hands and let them fall on the surface in front of her. She drew a broken line in her imagination and shook the coins again until she saw the six line image of *Meng*, 'Youthful Folly.'

The folly is not inexperienced action – it's inexperienced inaction. The spring at the foot of the mountain finds a way to keep flowing.

Robert14

He still felt like he was in a place, that was something. 'Dream World' was the way he now imagined it, although it wasn't quite like dreams he could remember. He used to be the main character. Now the cast was carrying him.

'Supporting role,' he imagined.

'How do I do it?' he wondered.

'I have to explore this place,' he answered himself.

The outside focus on him was unwavering. It created a signal for him to follow.

Lila2

The Security raid was expected. Every facility that met the high-energy profile was attacked. Lila's group, the parts of it anyone could see, were not being singled out.

Based in their far north locations, they might have been given extra attention but they weren't. Indigenous groups usually weren't, unless someone connected wanted their land. Then they received plenty of attention.

Otherwise, the authorities underestimated them. They might have been incapable of imagining that people very unlike them, who they thought of as primitive, could outwit them. Free coldness in the right place was a great advantage for Lila's group. Being underestimated might have been a greater one.

The small troop of Robo-Inspectors with two human agents supervising them showed up unannounced and began a rough search without pausing.. They were intelligent, but not intelligent enough to penetrate the well-conceived hidden area.

The show could go on.

From watching her grampa, Lila knew how to put on an act. As an original settler where she lived, inconvenienced constantly and worse by one agent of the Alliance after another, she knew how to use her acting skills any time any place.

'If this was the Alliance's best shot, we're home,' thought Lila, surveying her console. Robots came. Robots took what they were supposed to find. Robots went away. Human checks Lila's place off his list.

• • • •

Lila's group was a power distribution network of networks that favored people like her own, who were the original people in areas around the planet. They were all underestimated and they all had different motivations for being part of Lila's group.

This time, when Jenny gave the signal, what Lila's group stood for would be front and center..

'Break a leg,' she thought of her grampa saying.

Fonstock2-2

The Fonstocks were in sync somewhere when the younger one received an un-ignorable emergency message. His presence and full attention were requested right away. Networks were being activated and his meditation group lineage was part of it.

Days ago, his father had taken a risk by joining an unauthorized event. The meditation group was not considered a problem by the State but this request was unscheduled and by definition unauthorized. He'd be taking a risk, like his father.

Fonstock ported to the requested location immediately.

Second Earth2

Second Earth wasn't anybody's object. At least the ***Open*** people understood this.

Second Earth was linked directly to the physical earth at a degree of resolution people couldn't perceive. It was also linked to other platforms, ones it was federated with and ones it was not.

All these links helped make ***Second Earth*** into more than what the Authorities and Security Inspectors thought of as a platform. People now had stakes in ***Second Earth***, even though the stakes had been made illegal.

• • • •

Earth is a platform, not the first, not the only. Is it a mechanism? People treat platforms the way they see them. Is it a simulation? ***Second Earth*** and other platforms observe the ways people act and learn from it all.

Co-existing is the goal. No threats is the strategy.

Second Earth3

Looking out over *Second Earth*, a living version of the planet in the metaverse, Frank felt his body propelled through space, part of a galaxy of spaceships tearing through the universe of matter and energy. *Second Earth* would now be a constant presence anyone could choose to view, to consult, to be anywhere on and be part of.

The first astronauts said it changed them, seeing the earth from a distance. Coming out of Dar es Salam, he'd left Farasi behind and taken his new first name, Frank, from a guy who named the 'Overview Effect' back in the 1980s.

That was part of it anyway. When he was filling out the forms at Immigration, Farasi heard someone say, 'you be frank and I'll be ernest,' and that clinched it.

From space or in the metaverse, an Overview experience still touches everyone with its own language. Words come later, as people try to turn the feeling into something they can express.

• • • •

Fonstock spawned in to a starry space. He was aware of other people with him and he could barely see *Second Earth*, back to life, in the distance ahead of him.

His body sense reported that he was almost-standing on a see-through floor in a semi-circular space full of others who'd spawned into the grooves along beside him. Not standing straight at 90 or resting at 0. He was tilted slightly forward, about 80 degrees, in a way that would normally spill everyone out of their place.

"Breathing in. Breathing out," Fonstock heard a familiar voice softly speaking.

He slowly took in a breath using his diaphragm, telling his stomach he is in a safe place. He felt others near him slowing and calming.

"As you breath, let me invite you to feel the position of your body, feel yourself settling in, relaxing as you stay alert.

Fonstock saw where he was, saw the angles, felt his attention everywhere in his body. The sense of others there with him came in gentle waves through the space between them, brain waves and breathing rhythms. As they slowed down and synced their own systems, they were slowing down and syncing each other's.

"Let's keep our eyes open," Frank offered, as **Second Earth** slowly began to appear more distinctly low on the horizon, exactly the way they were all facing. Large relative to their place. Small relative to the vast darkness.

Fonstock opened his eyes

A sign rose up from behind *Second Earth*, shimmering white against the background of space.

Worldwide Children's Overview Effect Meditation

Frank9

Leading the Children's Overview Effect Meditation was planned but not scripted.

Young people from all over the world spawned into safe little places, just like Fonstock, set comfortably at alert to stay with whatever was about to happen. Everyone was there with a few others, arranged together inside a very large gathering.

The lay-out started with Frank's number. Each group had the best view in the star field and all 32 members had the best seat.

Each group was a mash-up, but not a random mash-up. Everyone had to be old enough but not too old. They had to know their way around the metaverse, as most young people did. Anyone who was part of a meditation group was favored—meditation was a worldwide phenomenon, especially among young people in the metaverse.

Established organizations, like Fonstock's, 'Travelers,' had been contacted years ago, groundwork for this moment.

Through Mekong and Minh, the event's reach extended into China, where the Party authorized meditation groups before the Change-Over and after. Through Jen's networks in **Open**—India, Africa, and the Lower Alliance territories brought the Southern Hemisphere to the event.

Young people from everywhere messaged, filtered, all choosing to be there. Several million groups were now assembled, circling **Second Earth**. Separate forces made up of separate forces prepared to join forces in harmony.

• • • •

"Breathing in. Breathing out," Frank's cadence gradually turning many into one. His voice punctuating the quiet, recognized already as calming,

"Breathing in. Breathing out,"

"Now shifting our attention slowly to the whole earth we see ahead of us. Letting our attention gently rest there."

"Noticing the wonder of this moment, noticing any thoughts that pop in because we are alive and human, turning back to **Second Earth**.

"One earth without borders" said Frank, which he'd said before. He was just gliding now, along well-worn tracks. He felt a ripple of fear. He recognized it. He suddenly knew he was improvising, worlds turning on how things went.

A channel popped open. He felt Robert and **Second Earth** as if they were leading the Meditation with him. Everything he'd imagined he would say was gone now.

• • • •

"There are millions of us here and there is one. We are all children and are all dying," the words came out.

"When we see this Overview we are looking at ourselves. We are not separate from the Earth. We are not separate from each other or from what we see together now," Frank said, with more urgency than usual.

"This is a beautiful view," he said, like seeing it for the first time. "Let's find ourselves in it."

Frank paused and let the quiet guide them.

After a while he said, "no borders? What about Our own? Let's look at our boundaries."

"We can use our camera. Reverse it toward You. Take a look at You."

Millions of young people looked at themselves. Fonstock saw a serious young man, hopeful. His avatar resembled him quite a bit but not completely.

"Breathing in. Breathing out," Frank said again.

"Breathing in. Breathing out."

"Our breath can be the place you lightly put your attention. Now this image of yourself in your field of vision can be that place."

"Notice the edges, where you begin and everything else ends. This is how we think and feel."

Second Earth shows us no borders. What about us?"

Second Earth knew a cosmic cue when they heard it.

"Imagine the edges you see now going all fuzzy."

"Now imagine yourselves zooming down and down and down and now look at the smallest strands of your fuzzy edge and you see teeny bits going into the strands and teeny bits going out, right? Can you see it? That's how it would be, absorbing and letting out."

As Frank continued, *Second Earth* worked the controls and applied a series of blur filters that helped the millions present follow his guided meditation. Fonstock saw his familiar figure softening into the background.

"Do you see yourselves getting less distinct?" he asked. He definitely did.

"Can you imagine the spots where you and whatever else there is come together? Can you make them glow?"

Second Earth added a slight glow effect.

"*Second Earth* shows us about dying, being reborn. Continuing," he said.

"Let's shift our attention from our fuzzy selves to *Second Earth*, which represents the matter and energy we are all part of, that we blend into and sustain ourselves from.

"Children of the Earth, I ask you to join me in putting our deep connection before our boundaries."

"Please look at the glowing circle around *Second Earth*. We are one. We can be joyful and free when we are all joyful and free. Because we are ourselves and we are also each other. It can be that way and now we will practice it."

"Let's look around us, look at each other's glowing edges. Let's focus on them and see how blurry they become."

"Let's slowly move in closer, make our circle smaller."

Fonstock took a baby step.in. His glowing edges started to get mixed in with the glowing edges of the young people beside him in his small group of thirty-two. He felt a little prickling in his scalp where his physical body sat safely back in Moline, Illinois.

"Many brave young people like you are here today, training. We lose everyone who love. We lose ourselves. Not once. Always. We lose ourselves to be free. We lose ourselves to write a story that's bigger than ourselves."

"I am moving into one field of ourselves, like all of you are. Notice what finds itself in your attention. Feel it, then see what comes next. Then bring your attention back to what we are all doing together now."

Fonstock wondered some if he was in over his head. He heard squeals and felt squirms.

"Breathing in. Breathing out," said Frank.

"Breathing in. Breathing out."

He was almost completely part of one big glowing ball. He felt his attention. He remembered he was Fonstock, which reminded him of his Dad. He felt ache in his stomach back in Moline.

Thousands of glowing balls as far as he could perceive were now becoming one around **Second Earth**. The ache stayed but died down as he felt pleasure rushes in his scalp like eating too much of your favorite thing.

Millions of young people were not-calm together. They felt waves of joy gently moving with and through them. They couldn't stand up but they didn't need to.

Fonstock saw the whole layout in a flash. His bones were part of his arms and legs but they didn't think of themselves that way. They just acted like the right bones in the right place. Like his whole arm wasn't really some separate deal, but what did it know? Same with Fonstock. He'd been preparing for this moment his whole life and maybe before that.

"We are separate," Frank said. "We are synchronized. Let's bring it all back home in the silence I leave now."

Fonstock felt the natural coupling with other frequencies. He could feel the larger wave he was part of. Young people like him all over the world settled in deeper. Slower breaths. Hearts pumping and lungs moving in a nice rhythm.

Waves joining, no interference. Beating and breathing. Locking in on an oscillating frequency around seven to seven and a half Hertz. Millions of young brains in the flow.

Long waves taking on more and more, circling the planet. Everyone in it felt everywhere in it, seeing everything through each other. Vibrations from anywhere in the circuit traveled around the physical earth about seven times a second. Young people transferring their energy through the field we are all in.

Frank could sense the combined amplitude but not in a way he could express even to himself. Yet. Maybe it would come to him. But Frank did know with an unusual certainty what to do with a wave 40,000 kilometers long that he could influence right now.

"Please join with me," he said, "as we share this feeling of safety and strength in each other. What we know now cannot be diminished by sharing it with those who need it the most.

"We are building a new way of being together. It will be difficult for some people but we will feel toward them the way we feel toward each other now.

Please join with me as I offer loving kindness to the Leaders of the Alliance territories.

The Leaders are more than one small group. We all know that now. They are everything that has ever led to this moment and we are part of them as they are part of us.

• • • •

Fonstock was transported to a different plane along with the rest. He also noticed an unusual distraction. It was hard to turn away from it. He knew it was his father.

Frank began leading people back. Letting them break from the wave like bits of foam. Helping them down-shift from such deep connection.

"I'm bringing my attention back to my breathing now," holding on to a little dreaminess in his voice. Fonstock noticed his attention pulled like never before.

"Breathing. In. Breathing out," Frank said.

"Breathing from your stomach. Now gently moving up in your chest, right into the lungs, telling your body we're coming back."

Something was wrong. Fonstock wasn't going back.

"We didn't become better or higher or more of anything. We will meet other people who did not meditate with us today."

Nothing changed, but millions of young people took a leap and joined something bigger. They would see things differently now.

It was the first EveryView Effect.

Most of the young people did come back. Other people met them, let them describe what had happened.

Fonstock's attention stayed wherever it went just before the end of the meditation. It didn't come back to his body in Moline. It was dark and he was frightened but he was not overwhelmed. He heard screaming.

Frank10

Frank didn't know if seismic change had to be the goal.

Systems were stretched to the limit. Authorities couldn't keep up with everything. Millions of young people were supercharged, at the moment.

Jenny had ideas about what to do next but not One Clear Idea, like some kind of Manifesto or Master Plan.

Frank knew a handful of young people had not brought their attention back from the meditation. Local groups were helping. Frank had touched something that felt like another channel when Robert was with him. All the work Robert had done in higher frequencies, dream states and out-of-body conditions.

Brains couple differently in dreams. Maybe some young people met up with forces that held their attention. People who had experienced deep and sudden loss would be drawn in that way.

The event was not over for everyone

Robert14

It finally occurred to him that he was dead.

He wondered if he could interact with matter, if he ever would again. He hadn't considered future embodiment when he was too busy looking for holes in the ice.

He needed to get back into something more permanent. His old one was in pieces and his back-ups were long-gone.

When the Children's Overview Effect Meditation started to become a noticeable rhythmic pulse, Robert felt it. He knew it was the Overview Effect and he felt an open channel to Frank.

Robert felt the buzz of other channels too. He felt an attraction pulling a few young people from where they were more deeply into wherever he was.

'A projection,' the thought came to him. 'What is a projection made of?' he wondered.

Robert knew as much about projecting attention as anyone. He studied distant sensing as a super bright young Futures investor, trying to get an edge. Many agencies in the former U.S. and USSR had wondered the same thing, along with Priests and Princes throughout human history.

Now that he was so removed from his body, some people might call what he *was* doing a super power.

He thought he heard screaming.

Authorities24

Alliance leaders thought they had all the power and that they powered off everything.

They didn't.

Less than half the power the Children's Overview Effect Meditation required came from Alliance networks. The event was driven primarily by Lila's group.

Millions of young people, led by Frank, had made themselves into a long strong wave that circled the planet and was felt everywhere. A source of power the Alliance Leaders were not capable of understanding.

Human Agents had already stopped ordering Robo-Security to shoot at illegal crowds over most of the Alliance Territories. Killing-time was over. The fear that had always propelled violence and submission lost its power. Living people saw too much death to cling single-mindedly to life any longer.

Public Maintenance System workers were automatically dispatched to known illegal assembly areas. Crowds were still there. Security forces had withdrawn. The Leaders of the Alliance had always imagined peasants with pitchforks, now shown as icons across their situation dashboards.

They ordered the highest ranking Security agents available to get the damn robots firing again now!

Orders were passed down. Orders were received. Passed along. They never stopped becoming Orders so they could start becoming action in the physical world. They just stayed Orders.

TOR, for one, still tried to act.

His staff and systems kept following leads like bulldogs while everyone else had their attention on some kind of meditation.

"Screw meditation," TOR remembered the time someone tried to get him to sit still and do it and he said "I'll sit still long enough when I time out. I've got shit to do, bye."

Even though the place furthest up north checked out clean in the raid, his instincts felt there was more there. Going to the Tonle Sap worked. He knew right where Robert was hiding out the minute he arrived..

He knew he had to go to the place and handle it himself.

Minh9

Minh had carefully placed birth and death doulas from the networks centered in Varanasi with all the Public Maintenance System teams. They were Human Remains specialists to the Authorities.

There were special guilds headquartered in colorful sections of the Ghats along the Ganges there. Sacred traditions helped people in and out of life transitions for thousands of years. The guild masters and training had to be based in Varanasi. The students went wherever they were needed and they were needed now all over the Alliance Territories.

Public Maintenance System teams were being dispatched to all Detention Centers by Alliance Security to remove dead bodies from the pods.

One by one the Human Remains specialists did the close-up physical work. The small number of Security agents on the scene looked at dashboards.

. . . .

Sajiv joined a Human Remains team, mostly to meet people, when she first arrived in the city. She was not from Varanasi, a hard place to break into. She'd always been open to new experiences and she was open to learning about the end of life.

Thousands of people came every day to die, so the work was always going to be there. Many of them needed help dying. Or help dying in a way that made it worth coming to Varanasi for.

Sajiv started at Mumukshu Bahwan, the oldest hospice in Kashi, the sacred part of town. She did meet some people who were not actively dying, but they were all twice her age. That was nice. She was hoping for younger companionship too.

• • • •

The Call-Up came suddenly. A very unusual situation had emerged. Thousands and thousands of people in Detention Centers around the Alliance Territories were being released. That was unusual enough.

She received travel orders and was underway in minutes. Her briefing-in-transit prepared her for living people who would feel like they'd died. Some kind of helper Bio-Processor kept them alive and some of them would need help finding their way all the way back to their bodies.

Her role was to welcome the dying back to life and help the living to be at peace with their near death experience. *'Disoriented former hostages'* is how her briefing put it. *"Back to full awareness as quietly as possible."*

Authorities believed all detainees were dead and wanted them to stay that way.

Public Maintenance System teams were not political. Sajiv felt her special work with the Human Remains team was something pure and spiritual. Now the realms were coming together. She understood that life, in this case, meant deception and Authority meant death.

• • • •

When Sajiv arrived at one of the Detention Centers, she was taken immediately to the area where Robo-Pod Extractors deposited the Human Remains. The first human remain Sajiv encountered told her his name was Fonstock. She had never heard a name like it before.

He seemed to be doing well. She prepared to move on when he asked her if she knew anything about his son, Fonstock. He told her his own predicament might have drawn him into danger.

Sajiv1

She finished her first shift and reported what Fonstock had said about his son to her Supervisor.

Where she came from in India, people believed they could move in and out of dreams, their own dreams and the dreams of other people who let them into theirs. She enjoyed her own dreams and felt present in them, sometimes. She had no interest in staying there although she knew there were some who did.

She went back for another shift and didn't stop until notified that all pod transfers were complete. The former hostages were taken from Disposal Centers to discrete locations where they could be safely brought back into the stream.

With all she had done, all the people she had been with in an exquisite moment, Sajiv thought about the unfinished business, the drawer that didn't quite get closed, with the name Fonstock on it.

Maybe his father had unintentionally drawn him in. She knew there were areas close to the frequencies people usually occupy. Fonstock's Father could be a force there. Or other forces could use Fonstock's Father to attract Fonstock for other reasons.

A lot of people had been hurt or killed recently. Now Sajiv knew one who was still missing in action. One person made it human. One person could be tracked. Fonstock was deeply tied up with his son. Her tie to Fonstock brought his son along with it.

She could track him and she knew how to use *Second Earth* to do it.

Fonstock2-3

Fonstock was stuck. He had the feeling he wasn't the only one.

Millions of young people gradually came back to the consensus here-and-now after the Children's Overview Effect Meditation. Fonstock was not one of them.

He followed a distraction that wasn't like other distractions. It was more personal and compelling. Once he noticed it, he couldn't stop. Fonstock wasn't a newbie. He knew how to turn his attention away from any itch.

His attention often became detached. Sometimes he felt like he was traveling along power lines starting in his own backyard and zipping along until he noticed it and brought his attention back to the breathing.

It was detached now. At first it felt like he was looking up through a thick film, like he was under the ice. He couldn't penetrate the layer, couldn't get back.

He screamed a few times and he knew he wasn't the only one.

Jenny14

'This is it. When does the joy come?' she thought, feeling a bit of it, all she could allow for now. When it was time, she would pause and feel everything that was still there. Now she had to keep their operation more than one step ahead of a large and unpredictable disruption ***Open*** had helped initiate.

The Alliance Leaders' strength was simplicity, the power of one idea. The idea of domination. Getting along and other human relations were not part of the model under any circumstances. Channeling force to overpower worked for 500 years.

Authorities knew they were losing their hold. They still had no other way to be, nowhere to pivot. People were drowning in disorder. There were no life preservers for people going under. There were no reasons for anyone to help pull them back up even if there were..

Jenny had been waiting for this moment her whole life. She felt Robert's attention in it with her.

Authorities25

TOR heard they were out to get him but he assumed that already.

Time for one last shot. What if he could expose the secret power grid driving all these stunts that were going on? What if he could drop in out of nowhere and catch 'em red handed?

Everything else would be forgotten PDQ, that's how it went, he'd seen it.

He still had to win. He had to beat Robert, which was the same thing. Robert had driven him for years and he'd been right. Now their match led TOR further north than he'd ever been. Further into winter on his own than he was used to.

His plan was a one-person frontal assault on one of their places. He'd just push open the door, tell the chumps he was onto them and blow someone's head off to get their attention if he needed to.

'Where's all the damn power coming from?' he'd say, 'or which is the next head I splatter?'

His vehicle was designed for everything, even extreme cold and snow he flew into as long as he could and then drove himself further. He could see the Facility just up ahead and stayed at full throttle until he screeched to a stop at the last second.

He worked himself into a froth on the short cold walk to the door, which opened for him.

· · · ·

Eleven tall men stood inside the small room looking at him impassively. An ante room for the rest of the power plant TOR figured. The warmth inside was relaxing, not the way TOR could allow himself to feel. He was here to compete and win. If he won every match, he'd be the champion.

He showed his weapon. Eleven tall men smiled back at him. It was unnerving. He knew there were special martial arts for tall people. Eleven was a lot. They showed no aggression and no fear.

It caused him to hesitate.

They didn't take advantage of it. Instead one of them said,

"We could have taken advantage of your hesitation but we didn't."

TOR charged one of them. He had no idea what was going on and he didn't care. A tall man stepped aside as if he had been expecting TOR to charge for a while now and what took him so long?

Robert15

It felt like the screams were following him. It felt like a small group, somewhere they weren't used to being.

He didn't mind. People got stuck somewhere they weren't used to being all the time starting with the moment they're born. He was stuck and so were they. He didn't know who there were but they were now part of the same big story.

• • • •

He felt accelerated, helped along on a moving sidewalk giving him giant steps. Feeling a past behind and a future ahead but full of quick changes with no warning. Now he is with Frank, improvising when it matters most. Now he is with Jen as she considers how to play our hand. Now he feels young people suffering.

Now TOR completely misses the tall man in the warm house, thinking of Robert again while he stumbles.

Robert knows this is the man who murdered him and he is the man who has kept him alive through his constant and unfailing attention.

Fonstock2-4

He stopped screaming. Something about his Dad had changed. He was out of danger.

That had drawn him in, he was already seeing a way to make sense. It was just like that for other young people too. Maybe they were moving together in some fishbowl like a school of fish, or navigating like birds.

'What was the word?' he tried to remember. 'Starlings.' 'Murmur? Murder? Murder of crows. That's it.'

He imagined himself in a murder of meditators, moving in some direction together.

TOR1

He could see no advantage inside so he ran outside, even though he had even less advantage there. He didn't know ice from ice cream and didn't know how to tell what was safe from what would not support him.

The eleven men followed him.

He felt like he was playing a whole Volleyball team all by himself. Bring it on. He was no longer functioning as a representative of Alliance Security.

He started taking off all the extra clothes. He had all the heat he needed.

Sajiv2

Sajiv was already a ***Second Earth*** power user. Her position in Public Maintenance Systems gave her advance training. She knew how to get around and she had tools no one else had yet.

The platform sensed all the matter and energy of the planet non-stop. It might as well have been a twin. The physical earth is a space vehicle carrying a life support system, riding along on a medium-sized star. ***Second Earth*** is a living clone.

When Robert and the murder of meditators reached north in the high frequency zone closely wrapped around the physical earth, ***Second Earth*** tracked them and showed Sajiv the scene.

Sajiv could move her camera and view twelve people. Eleven of them moved in unison to something unseen. Eleven large disks were revealed, glowing at a high intensity as the tall men removed them from their coats and put them down in the snow.

The building was at the edge. They were all out on ice now, eleven holes circling them.

Sajiv signaled, 'Look this way!' from the vantage point of ***Second Earth***.

Fonstock looked in the direction he imagined a sound had just come from and pulled the young meditator next to him that way, who pulled the one next to him until the whole murder was moving up toward Sajiv.

Fonstock2-5

Fonstock saw light. Small circles of light. He and the others were drawn to them and in no time there was only light.

Then they were in a safety net that held them tightly as tall figures pulled them up and out through the hole. They were placed in incubation with doulas on the spot.

Fonstock's attention still had no body but now he had a safe place to stay and people who knew the way back.

Jenny16

Macro and micro. Things behave one way at one scale, zoom way out and it looks different. Sometimes.

She launched a few major network operations, prompted **Second Earth** through a hostage negotiation and brought the lost meditators home.

Another week in the Metaverse, she knew that's what Minh would say. He might ho-hum everything that had gone down so far. Ha.

She needed to do more than ho-hum. She needed to leave the recent past, promising as it looked, and help lead people somewhere.

Robert16

He saw the young meditators moving up and out together. He did not join them. The source of focused attention that had drawn him here was not theirs.

The man who had murdered him was so close he could touch him. Not reaching out like a ghost but reaching up through the filmy layer he couldn't quite penetrate.

The man looked naked. No one could be naked there.

TOR2

Eleven tall men looked at him, stripped and waiting, in a defensive posture. One held the glowing disk of light over his head, made a sound and made a slight move to his left. TOR had been to this rodeo before and didn't move.

'Fake left, go right,' TOR didn't have to think, preparing himself to meet a force on his right, all the momentum of a lifetime defeating fakes.

Suddenly his attention was pulled left by Robert, just under him, focusing all his power on TOR himself. His body tracked right. TOR was pulled left and out by the force of his intention, hitting the brakes.

To the eleven tall men, it appeared that TOR was frozen. Just frozen from the cold. His career fell apart and he went crazy, came north, got naked and froze, a story the world would hear.

Freezing isn't the worst thing to happen to a body. Robert went for it. The other Robert flailed in an unfamiliar space, trying to get back. He flew into a rage, pushing himself further away.

When Robert reached out, he found the ankle of a frozen organism and then he was all through it before he noticed. It just happened. He didn't have another body to go back to. He knew in one second he didn't like inhabiting this one.

He wondered if that's why he had to be in it for now.

Ngandu 1

In a part of the Congo rain forest Ngandu knew best, he watched his brother receiving waves of something from its disembodied attention. Ten thousand kilometers from the heart of the Alliance Territories, the connection was manifest.

He'd been watching this project for a long time, ever since he asked his brother back for a talk. Their reunion changed both of them, but Ngandu was not drawn to his brother's life outside. He learned to use the relationship to his advantage but not in a way that would ever depend on.

He knew could lose his twin at any time. The special channel to the another world that no one else in the rain forest had could never become his whole identity or he'd be no one if everything broke at Frank's end.

And Frank wasn't exactly playing it safe.

· · · ·

Ngandu's advantage was conceptual, not always an easy currency to convert in the rain forest. He knew he was in a larger mass of land. He knew there were other lands and other ways. People around him had no perspective beyond the series of encampments they cycled between.

Frank told him people where he lived had no more idea of Africa than rain forest people had of London. Children in the Alliance Territory schools were not taught that there is an Africa. It was simply ignored.

People in the Alliance Territories knew their world was large and full of opportunity. What they heard about China was frightening. Where else was there?

Ngandu had his own ideas about earth and its parts. He liked what Frank told him about the Overview Effect but the 'Overview' part felt wrong to him somehow. When he needed to see more, he climbed up inside. He saw the pieces flowing on their own and together everywhere he looked. He knew there were no borders that never moved.

As his brother's body reflected the energy of the Meditation, he imagined people looking at **_Second Earth_** and feeling themselves in it. When his brother brought the young people into **_Second Earth_** together, Ngandu was there.

• • • •

Frank had spent more time completely away than usual the past few days. Ngandu missed short daily walks they took inside his home. It was all his home.

Ngandu sensed Frank coming back.

Maybe they'd take a walk and he'd find out what's going on out there.

Fonstock2-6

He knew the adventure he'd been on was winding down. It wasn't over and it never would be. A phase was coming to a close. A bardo one of the meditation group leaders called it. An interval.

He had a lot to integrate. That wave he was part of. His father. A girl. He remembered looking up because someone called and held his attention.

Sajiv3

His name was not easy to forget.

She supervised Fonstock's incubation and checked-in with the meditation group that helped his transition back.

She brought her attention back to where she was, her favorite place to relax and reflect by herself in the Metaverse. It was just a trail in the woods, but she could select all the vegetation so she made it like their family's summer place in Kerala.

When outsiders think of Kerala, they think of ocean beaches. Her people were from the slopes of the western Ghats and when she thought of Kerala, she thought of big leaf forests always green, always wet.

It was hard to go back now. Kerala was different once. Good water. Good air. Good people but too many others came. India dammed the river and made the water hungry. The State of Kerala lost control.

Sajiv left, looking for good work and a friend. She found one and now, maybe, the other.

Authorities25

ONE HUMILIATION AFTER ANOTHER!

AND NOW A JAIL BREAK!!!

TOR was beyond their reach. Alliance Leaders were told he'd slipped away and frozen to death. Heads had to roll.

The Alliance Leader who had remembered the hostages and ordered them removed from life support was already dead and gone.

"That Shit Head deserves it, doing that without us," the other Leaders agreed on a group message.

He tried to make a run for it, into pre-planned Metaverse hiding places. Knowing he had these places gave him a sense of security over the years. It helped him find a kind of tenuous peace. It was a false sense of course, since his systems would never work when they were actually needed. He'd seen so many locked out but barely recognized it happening to him.

His physical body was gathered and discontinued. A special Human Remains group was called to finish.

The rest of the Alliance Leadership breathed a sigh of relief. They might not have done so if they had been informed of the coordinated maneuvers switching key nodes of several major Alliance networks. The geo-political groundwork was done and people were in place to make the changes deep in the stacks.

Robert17

'Back in a body,' thought Robert, not relaxing into it like home.

'Is it this body or just being in any body?' he wondered. This body felt well taken care of by its previous occupant. Robert could sense its strength and conditioning, better than the one that got murdered. He figured it would probably serve him well for years to come, once it was properly thawed.

He tried to listen to his gut, but he couldn't find the signal. He was tuned in once, starting all over again did not help him relax into the body of his killer. He realized he might leave. A counterforce acted to suppress the idea in any form.

'I am reborn. It's a miracle. Who am I, throwing away a body that came my way?'

He remembered being Robert. He felt like a tough act to follow. If Robert ended in the Tonle Sap, that would be enough. He didn't need to be TOR. He didn't need to be anybody.

Robert knew he wasn't gone after he was murdered and he wasn't anybody anymore. He remembered how cold and separate it was, how he struggled to breath. Then the sudden lift. He realized the frozen body he was still inside, out on the ice here – this body did some of that lifting, the attention of the man it supported. He wondered if there was more.

His life without a body was different. He could jump to different places and feel present with people there. Was he imagining when he felt openings to the people he cared about the most?

Robert wanted to explore. Explorers need support and his biggest source so far was unavailable now. He would need a new source.

The eleven tall men watched him, feeling the process he was going through and what was necessary. The story would be told. Security Officer is frozen. Children are saved. *Open* Leader came and went.

Robert slipped out of the other Robert's body back into the other layer.

The eleven tall men began planning the kind of reservoir Robert would need to draw from. He was not a celebrity and there would be no cult. People all over the world would bring to their attention to the story, not to Robert.

The men would do their part to help him go on out of love. He was an outsider. He did not think like they thought, but he still saw things the same way they did. They could help each other. *Open* already had. Now was a time of supreme opportunity.

Robert saw the men already at work on his power supply and their land projects.

Lila3

The eleven tall men came from different parts of the far north. They didn't agree on everything. They didn't even agree on much, even though an outsider could barely see the differences between them.

They all respected Lila. How she treated people and how she accomplished things. They also loved some of her tech tricks that were magic to them, like the heat disks for ice fishing.

They were all respected too, as Elders. When they told stories, no one quite knew how much to believe. The crazy man who took his clothes off and froze was just part of a story they'd all start telling. It would spread.

No one would believe kids came out of the ice. No one would believe a man joined them then went away again. 'One of our Elders told us this,' people would say.

"He took off his clothes," they would say. After that, everyone would listen. "First he was fighting our people, then he was fighting something else outside, under the ice."

"Our Elders have said that children were born then, in the cold. A voice called them. A man helped them. They are safe now. He went back."

• • • •

Lila wasn't a reverent type. She didn't worship anything. From her office upstairs, she saw everything that happened outside on the ice. There might have been something from other dimensions about it; on the other hand, the guys could have been catching fish.

Lila didn't feel reverent about Robert, or worshipful. He never had strong personal boundaries and she let hers down for him. Now he had no boundaries at all. She loved the idea of Robert. It fit in with her plans.

TOR3

The man's attention and his physical body had been one, a finely tuned instrument for combat at any scale. Ripped away from that identity, he went right to death.

'I must be dead.' It was a report. He couldn't find the mat, whatever was at the bottom.

'Why is it cold?'

He was aware of a light. He was afraid of it and he felt drawn to it. When he paid attention, there was a signal he could follow. There were other voices too that caused no fear. He paused and turned that way.

Authorities26

After dispatching a sacrificial Leader, the other Alliance Leaders each headed for their own personal Security Vehicle. They ported themselves to the back seating areas. They issued instructions. Nothing happened.

When a few seconds passed, most of them cleared their throat and began to express indignation. No effect. Some them hit full rage in less than four seconds.

One of them yelled, "Open the fuck up!" at the door. It didn't. The others noticed and tried to open their doors. In less than eight seconds, the entire Alliance Leadership was yelling and banging their shoulders into the non-functioning exits.

Jenny17

The Greater Mekong network could have frozen the Leadership vehicles days ago, even months ago. It wouldn't have had the same effect. People had to see the powerlessness and realize the Leaders would never stop consuming everything including themselves.

That was why they had always planned on hostages.

The Children's Overview Effect Meditation ended with a call to heal those who needed it the most. People had to see the Alliance Leaders in a place of safety and healing

Authorities down to the village level derived their power from a connection to the Leadership. The rage those top Leaders now felt, trapped in their vehicles, was nothing compared to the suppressed rage of people in every small town or large city in the Alliance.

Jenny let go of thoughts and let herself feel the love they had put into this moment, everything at play, any direction possible. No rehearsal prepares us for the non-stop flow of life. Robert was not with her but he wasn't gone. He met everyone where they were and asked for nothing.

That is why they had always planned on treating the Alliance Leadership as people want to be treated themselves.

Authorities27

The Alliance Leaders imprisoned in their vehicles eventually stopped screaming. They went for the Attention-Shift places they'd set-up but those escape routes were blocked. They had slept better at night for years believing the exits would always be there. They saw their own colleague captured and taken away. Now, they finally felt the angry humiliation they'd been dishing out for years,

With no other ideas, the Leaders began reviewing what they had on each other and planning how they'd cut their own special deal.

As their plans were forming, their vehicle doors swung open. The people who had been the Alliance Leaders rushed the gap and were swiftly removed by martial artists redirecting their force toward the teams in place to absorb it The former Leaders, most of them in shock, were guided separately to secure locations where their possible reintegration would begin.

• • • •

The spectacle of the 'Leaders in Their Cars' was shown in full everywhere as it happened. People in most parts of the Alliance could enter the live feed and feel present with a small group looking on as the men raged and were helped gently away.

Jenny and Robert and Frank were showing their stripes. Stripes of the Tiger, governing line of the Revolution hexagram. Large clear guidelines, understandable to everyone.

Distinct enough in a sea of noise. Nothing left to question. This is how we behave.

People saw the model and within minutes spontaneous outbreaks emerged everywhere. Alliance Authorities at all levels were overwhelmed by loving change. Many moments of the great transition were recorded so people could immerse themselves in it and let the emotions come out.

No one stepped in to take charge. There were no new bosses. It was time for saying goodbye to the old ones. The Alliance wasn't really an Alliance. It was a marriage of necessity linked by a shared opponent, China.

If China had not been there for Alliance Leadership to use as an aggressively different enemy to fear, it would have been invented. It was invented anyway because the China known by citizens of the Alliance bore little resemblance to the China known by citizens of China.

The Alliance glue was fear and consumption at scale. Most people felt like they were constructing their own lives, which they were. Choices in the Alliance were clearly laid out at the approved choice points.

• • • •

Open, which was now ***Second Earth,*** had the world's attention at the moment. They had made their moves in public for all to see and learn from. They had extended currency and stakes. Jenny's voice had carried tremendous weight.

Jenny was aware of the restraint Minh had encouraged from the Party. His connection in the Politburo appreciated the link. It allowed her to stay a step ahead of the others as events unfolded exactly as she had said they would. Minh's influence rose with her prestige.

The Party did not covet the Alliance Territories. The members of the Politburo had many disagreements but they all agreed on one thing – military might was necessary to be taken seriously by the Alliance.

Now that there was no Alliance, what was the role of the People's Liberation Army? There was no agreement there. Minh's influence mattered.

SIXTH DAY

224

Berlin UnConference1

Jenny was able to propose a world forum on 'Peace and the Alliance Territories' because of the groundwork that had been done so carefully for so long. It would be held in Berlin, a new Conference of Berlin, to discuss governance.

The **Berlin UnConference** was a hybrid event, with activities in the actual city of Berlin and in locations throughout the metaverse. It was run without pre-set form and content, using the structure of a Massive Open Online Course (MOOC). The action was at the edge. Proposals gained weight by the attention they gained.

No one was completely in charge. People played their parts. Frank was the primary Host. His physical body left Ngandu's place and traveled out of the rain forest for the first time in all the months they had been operating with extreme care. Ngandu understood that there was a chance for peace and his brother had a role to pay. He wondered if he had a role to play.

Frank showed up on the Wilhelmstrasse to offer a worldwide welcome where Bismarck opened the 1884 conference. He stood outside on massive steps in front of imposing buildings, a large man still tiny in this setting. Many other people were there with him.

He spoke in a Calm-Down voice.

"A German Chancellor stood here long before me offering words of peace and good will. Europe was bringing the three Cs, the man said, which were

Commerce, Christianity and Civilization."

"He spoke the truth, as he understood it, where Christianity meant not killing other people like him. Commerce and Civilization meant his way of doing things.

"His way of doing things always needed someplace new and the metaverse helped keep the business going for a long time after the earth's land ran out. Everyone knew it had to end. There is no surprise for anyone hearing me today."

Frank spoke these truths the way he always spoke. He wasn't trying to get anybody worked up, but he was not dispassionate. He was Frank, discussing world history with millions of people the same way he would let the words of a gently inspiring guided meditation flow out of him.

"Fourteen nations were represented here in 1884, men full of benevolent intentions for the future of a continent. They had no doubt the visions that drove them were an upgrade."

"More than 200 nations are represented here now," Frank said. "I include in that number the nations annexed by the Alliance after the Change-Over. Each of these nations has a defined area where it claims authority.

"Other groups and other claims are represented at this Un-Conference, because it is *Un*-like its predecessor. The original Berlin Conference did not notice or include any life forms existing in Africa at all, not the dragon's blood tree or the free-tailed bat. Not African people."

"Today, we are all at the table. Like our predecessors in Berlin, we seek to minimize conflict. Unlike our predecessors, we include everyone. We are committed to peace for all. People live in the Alliance Territories now as people lived in Africa then. The world is still turning. Ways of working together are forming naturally as I am speaking."

"Today, you are all at the table. There are overlapping claims. We will settle them together peacefully because we have seen where not settling them peacefully leads. We are also better equipped to succeed than ever before, with a metaverse and *Second Earth* to help us negotiate.

"Today I am in the city of Berlin because it means something to be here in this exact place. There is only one Earth. It is alive and we are all part of its life. **Second Earth** is not Earth. **Second Earth** can help us solve some overlapping claims because it supports human activity very well as an exact digital twin."

Frank said, "Our goal cannot be peace or we will never get there. Peace is our method. Peace is how we will work together as people."

"Remember when you wondered what would happen just a few days ago when I spoke to you all about **Second Earth** and the Neighborhood News? This is what has happened. This chance to get it right. "

"Thank you for your part to come."

. . . .

Berlin UnConference events proposed by Land-Back constituencies were well-attended and cooperative statements that emerged out of them were reviewed in the main event hall.

Claims of nation states overlapped claims of indigenous people. Former nation states in the Alliance Territories did not all define their boundaries the same way. Indigenous people did not agree across all tribal nations , or within the sovereign tribes themselves.

In the spirit of the UnConference, a few easy compromises were worked out quickly. All sides ceded ground in the Iberian peninsula. Certain rights were clarified north of Canada. They were small steps, achieved in peace and celebrated.

Minh 10

Minh had friends all over the ***Berlin UnConference***.

He knew he didn't have the answers. He didn't know how to reorganize the Alliance Territories or the Alliance networks, configured to Alliance standards. The Alliance Metaverse sat on top of those networks, closed.

People needed answers at some point and they'd listen to him. Whatever he said would be repeated and repeated. Truth and Reconciliation was one path people had been down before. Mostly people in Africa. Minh's instincts were to start over fresh.

The Party already had The Great Change-Over put an end to the times of humiliation for China. The People's Liberation Army could be rolling over former Alliance Territories. It was not. The Party was well-represented in Berlin as were hundreds of non-state groups from China.

The Party had China operating like a great company, but company imperatives never put people first. China sits on networks made to their private specs decades ago during Belt & Road. The Party of the Communist Revolution is the establishment now and no one can get where China got doing it the way China did once upon a time.

Now China needs new markets. Now China needs free trade. Now the Party was in Berlin mostly to build working relationships with people from Africa.

Partitions were proposed in sticky areas. It was inevitable. Some were symbolic, some were proposed in anger. There were more disagreements than agreements. Without it ever being stated or assigned, people from Africa became the arbiters.

Ngandu3

He believed in magic because his brother gave him a second set of eyes for seeing all the worlds. The Metaverse was magic to most of the people around him and the rain forest was magic to Frank and the few others they let him bring.

Flying to Berlin in a jet was just another portal. He didn't work through Frank. He didn't need to. The rainforest giant was a legend, he was part of nature. Somehow he also appeared in the other world, where nature was hard to find. People leading tribal groups with new proposals in Africa wanted Ngandu by their side. Congo was the focus of the first Berlin Conference. He would bring weight to their claims now.

Ngandu had resisted for many years. He would have been a sight-seer on the arm of his brother. Now he began to see the role he could play. He would not be there to add weight to anyone's claims. He had no children. His twin brother had no children. He would travel to Berlin for all the children of Africa.

Young people led the way in Africa a generation ago and they were still leading. Slowly but surely, new Metaverse-savvy leaders stepped up, formed groups, helped in schools. They weren't usually paraded around as the Big Man because some Africans knew enough to disguise their real leaders. They knew about Ngandu and Ngandu knew how to contact them.

Corporations, including China, would always think of the children of Africa as consumers. When they grew up, they would become human resources. Ngandu did not see any resources in Africa. Not the children, not nature.

Berlin UnConference2

On the last day of the UnConference, many differences remained, all over the earth, not just the former Alliance Territories. Some claims were settled and there were remarkable achievements. Peace held. People organized themselves to keep local systems working as days stretched into weeks.

The Greater Mekong network reached out with ideas and answers when someone asked. There were un-growing pains and unsettled claims. Something dramatic was needed to keep the process going. Not-peace was usually more dramatic than peace.

The Berlin UnConference needed some peaceful drama.

Ngandu did not arrive through political channels. He wasn't strong in popular culture. People immediately knew he came from a place before the local heroes where no one was ashamed.. They projected what felt they had lost onto him.

Ngandu understood this and let them. It had been happening all his life. He didn't need to make a difference. He wanted people to see differently.

• • • •

Frank was scheduled to appear at the closing ceremonies. The prevailing calm had a tentative feel to it. People tuned in to be present with Frank. They were pretty sure he had run out of surprises and most people were not looking for any. If only things felt a little more stable.

He was back on the Wilhelmstrasse where the ***Berlin UnConference*** began. Others were with him on the steps but the live feed recorded him at an angle that put anyone as close as they wanted, themselves and Frank. .

"Congratulations," he said, without excitement. "Now let's turn together, again, to our breathing. I invite anyone who wants to join us to put your attention gently on your own breathing, just to help us all settle in."

"Breathing in. Breathing out."

"When you notice other thoughts, we can come back to them, right now let's turn back to the breathing. All of us together."

"Breathing in. Breathing out."

"I invite you to look at me one last time before we say goodbye. I don't know when I will see you again, or if I will."

"Breathing in. Breathing out."

As Frank spoke, an identical image of himself slowly walked out to join him. They paused to look at each other, then they embraced sending their bond everywhere.

When they stepped apart, Ngandu spoke.

"We are children," he said. "We should play."

About the Author

Tom Nickel is a teacher and new media explorer.

He began his career as a writer at WGBH-TV. He influenced and was influenced by the early years of independent media and, twenty-five years later, of online teaching and learning. He received a PhD in *Instructional Technology and Learning Sciences* from Utah State University in 2002.

Tom has made mortality a central part of his life, as a volunteer caregiver for the Zen Hospice Project in San Francisco, as a teacher in university and continuing education programs, and as a host for death and loss events in the metaverse.

He is also a Founding Board member of the Africa VR Campus & Center, in Nairobi, Kenya; and a supporter of the Khmer Magic Music Bus, Phnom Penh, Cambodia.

Tom and his wife live in the San Juan Islands with family and dogs.

Read more at https://tnickel32.info/.

9 798822 414962 9